VINTAGE

APERTURE

Bhaskar Chattopadhyay is an author and screenwriter. He started his career by translating Bengali and Hindi writers such as Rabindranath Tagore, Premchand and Bibhutibhushan Bandyopadhyay. He now writes mystery fiction and thrillers. He has also written several books on film-maker Satyajit Ray. Bhaskar's first feature screenplay releases in October 2024. He lives in Toronto with his wife and two sons and teaches screenwriting at York University.

A Janardan Maity Mystery

Bhaskar
Chattopadhyay

VINTAGE
An imprint of Penguin Random House

VINTAGE

Vintage is an imprint of the Penguin Random House group of companies
whose addresses can be found at global.penguinrandomhouse.com

Published by Penguin Random House India Pvt. Ltd
4th Floor, Capital Tower 1, MG Road,
Gurugram 122 002, Haryana, India

First published in Vintage by Penguin Random House India 2024

10 9 8 7 6 5 4 3 2 1

ISBN 9780143464235

Typeset in Garamond by MAP Systems, Bengaluru, India

www.penguin.co.in

To Ishaan,

May you always have the strength to choose the light

[1]

'Magic is dying, my friend,' said Janardan Maity.

It was just after nine in the night. We had walked out of the Mahajati Sadan Auditorium on Chittaranjan Avenue, flagged down a cab and settled down in our seats, the gentle night breeze from over the river in the west just managing to provide some much-needed relief from the sweltering heat of June. I was admiring the line of handcarts arranged neatly along the side of the footpath near Muhammad Ali Park, when Maity let out a sigh and uttered those dismal-sounding words.

'Right in front of our eyes,' Maity continued, 'and we aren't doing a thing about it.'

We had just come out after watching a magic show. The magician was a young up-and-coming illusionist whom the papers had given rave reviews. Good magic was a rarity in Kolkata these days—most of the performances were cheap parlour tricks that wouldn't even impress children, and the rest depended so heavily on glamour and machinery that it sort of ruined the fun. At least that's what Maity said. During tonight's show, I had glanced at Maity a couple of times to find that he was not at all impressed by the quality of the tricks being played out on stage by the young man who had clearly focused more on trying to look like Mandrake than on his sleight of hand. But I could also see as easily that Maity really wanted to enjoy the show, that he was trying his best to do so—and failing hopelessly. With the announcement of every trick, he would sit up straight, in anticipation of a baffling enigma, an awe-inducing miracle, but when the cymbals would crash and the trick would be complete, Maity would sink back in his seat like a deflated balloon, disappointed and dejected. This went on for three full hours.

'In Europe, Australia, even in the Americas, there are so many schools that are completely dedicated to teaching the art of circus. Theatre and fine arts are being taught widely. There is at least an effort to preserve these old arts, either in their original, ancient forms or in their contemporary avatars. But magic? No, there's no school of magic you can go to in order to learn the good old illusion. Schools of magic remain only in fiction now, don't they? Every once in a while, you see an old, widowed lady on the footpaths of Kolkata somewhere, showing one wondrous trick after another. Coins, keys, cards, even stones and pebbles and toothpaste caps, Prakash! Toothpaste caps! Can you believe it? Nothing else, no fancy apparatus, no dazzling lights, no screens, no assistants, not a single word of patter uttered to distract the audience. Just a few ordinary items, and ten wrinkled brown fingers creating magic. *True* magic! All for a square meal at the end of the day.'

The hurt in Maity's voice was unmistakable. Not once while saying these words had he looked at me. His sight was fixed outside the cab's window, on the streets, and although I could not see his face, the choke in his voice told me that it was accompanied by a glisten in his eyes. Bhowanipore was a fair distance away; I was staying over at Maity's for the night, and I couldn't obviously let him go through the rest of the evening lamenting, so I tried to steer the conversation towards another direction, with the express objective of lifting his mood. It took some doing, but gradually, it seemed to work. I spoke about a new plot that was bouncing around in my head. Maity heard it with some attention, and gave me a few suggestions which I thought were extremely useful. I asked him if he had ever considered writing, and he responded by claiming that he lacked the discipline to do so. I was wondering if there was anything under the sun that Janardan Maity lacked the discipline to do and accomplish, when our taxi pulled up in front of Maity's ancestral mansion.

The door was answered by Maity's loyal and aged servant Mahadev, who informed us that a gentleman had been waiting to see us, and that although he had been duly informed that Maity would be late in returning home, he had repeatedly insisted—much to the chagrin of Mahadev—that he would wait. For, as he had claimed, the matter was of utmost importance.

When we stepped into the drawing room, the young man stood up to greet us. I would have described the man as pretty much ordinary-looking, but I knew how much Maity hated that description, so I quickly add that he was of medium height and build, wore an inexpensive shirt with the sleeves rolled up to his elbows and a pair of faded jeans, carried a black cracked and patched leatherette satchel on his left shoulder and wore a pair of flip-flops on his feet. His hair, all haphazard and poorly trimmed, had clearly not received a touch of oil over months, if not years. There was a thin moustache over his lips, and somehow it seemed to my eyes that on a regular day, he was a decidedly unkempt man, but that he had made an extra effort to dress up a little on the occasion of meeting the greatest detective of Kolkata, if not the country. I noticed that Mahadev had dutifully placed a cup of tea in front of the man, but from the thin, crusty film that had formed on the surface of the tea, it was obvious that the cup had remained untouched.

After we had taken our seats and Mahadev had brought us a glass of water each, Maity looked at the man with a gentle smile, without saying anything.

'My . . . I am actually a photographer, sir,' the man said, slightly raising his satchel. 'By profession, that is. My name is Sayantan Kundu.'

'*Actually*?' Maity said, with the hint of a question lacing his smile.

'Well . . . I . . . I mean . . .' The man hesitated.

Maity watched the man keenly for a second or two, then summoned Mahadev to take the tea away and bring three cups of coffee. Then he raised his right foot over his left and said: 'You seem pretty much the same age as my dear friend Prakash here. But I am an old-fashioned man, with old-fashioned tastes. I hope you wouldn't mind if I addressed you by your second name?'

'Oh no, certainly not, sir.'

'That is most generous of you. Now, Mr Kundu, I don't know if you would believe me, and let me assure you that I am not exaggerating one bit, but Prakash and I have had— let's just say—one of the most exhaustingly unrewarding experiences of our lives tonight. And for no fault of ours, I might add. Which is one of the many reasons why I would urge you to be frank with me, seeming as it does that meeting me is of some amount of importance to you.'

I glanced at the man feeling a little bad for him. Clearly, Maity's foul mood had accompanied him home, and the poor fellow had been caught right in the centre of the tornado. But the man seemed to gather his wits about him. He took a deep breath and began again.

'My name is Sayantan Kundu, sir. I am a photographer by profession. I learnt photography from my father, who used to run a small studio near Lake Market. After his death, the studio folded up—it wasn't doing well anyway; nobody comes to get their family photographs clicked in studios any more, and clicking passport photographs was not something I was interested in doing. So, I started specializing in celebrity photography. Became a paparazzo, if you will. But that field is quite crowded. Everyone has a high-end camera these days, and everyone claims to be a photographer, I'm sure you are aware of that.'

'I am,' said Maity patiently.

'There's just no money left in it any more, not unless you are willing to sell your soul, that is. Take photographs of celebrities at their most embarrassing moments, you know— wardrobe malfunctions, awkward gestures, revealing attire, a brawl, sometimes . . . sometimes a brawl that they have been forced into . . . the whole thing is just . . . just . . .'

'Wrong?' Maity suggested.

Sayantan Kundu nodded. Maity gently advised him to take a sip of coffee, as he sipped from his own cup and placed it with the saucer back on a low table next to his favourite couch.

'To be honest with you, I just wasn't being able to make ends meet,' Sayantan continued. 'Within a year of my father's death, my mother passed away. My elder brother left for Bangalore with his family; he was never interested in the family business and I have heard he has taken up a job there. The burden of my father's debt fell on my shoulders. I lost our ancestral house. It was not in good shape, but even then, it was worth at least thrice what my father owed in debt. But when the vultures are circling, nothing seems to work in your favour. Fate has not been kind to me, sir—I lost my home, my family, everything. I started doing odd freelance jobs here and there. Standing outside five-star hotels for hours in the rain. Waiting outside clubs and discotheques. Eden Gardens, the airport, film studios, day, night, heat, rain—there was just no end to it all. I rented a small apartment on the third floor of a house near Park Lane, sir. If it can be called an apartment, that is. Just a room with space enough for a bed and a chair and a stove. With a door leading to a filthy bathroom and a tiny window looking down on the damp and seedy lane below. Old derelict British-style building—I think it used to be a garment factory of some sort back in the day. Some Gujarati promoter named Parekh bought it in the 1980s and now one of his sons rents out pigeonholes to people who have no place to go.'

Sayantan Kundu paused briefly to catch his breath and take another sip of his coffee. Maity was a finicky man. There was a specific suiting and shirting shop in New Market from where he secretly bought his coffee, at an obscenely high price. I had asked him the source of the coffee on numerous occasions in the past, and never received a clear or credible response. But it did seem that our young photographer friend was now regaining some of his confidence fairly quickly.

'It had almost begun to seem to me that there was just no way for me to survive other than to sell my cameras. But then one day, lady luck smiled on me, sir! It was . . . I don't think I can find the right words to describe it to you . . . it was a miracle! Remember I told you there was a tiny window in my room? It was less of a window and more of a ventilator, hardly an arm's length in size and may be half of that in width. And it was shut tight, with tinted glass. Around a year or so ago, a cyclone hit the city. You may remember it caused heavy damage in the coastal areas. The havoc it wreaked over the city was no less significant. The glass on my tiny window shattered to bits. That's when I discovered the building across the lane below.'

I quickly shifted my glance towards Maity to find him sitting upright on his couch.

'It was a hotel, sir,' Sayantan continued. 'When I found out, I walked by its entrance. Nothing fancy. Name's Fairy Glen. Internet says two stars. Reviews are bad. Complaints of thin walls, stained sheets, stinking bathrooms, the usual. But for me, it was a gold mine. Because from my tiny window, I had a view of as many as six rooms of the Fairy Glen. And . . . I . . . I . . .'

As the young man stammered, Maity lay back on his couch and picked up his cup. There was a familiar sparkle in his eyes, one that always, always manages to set my heart racing. It meant that Maity had found an interesting puzzle. As I could see Sayantan Kundu struggle to find his next words, Maity finished his coffee in two satisfying sips, gently placed the cup at the exact centre of the table, looked straight at our guest and said in clearly enunciated words, 'It is from years of experience of dealing with people, Mr Kundu, that I have come to learn a thing or two about the human soul.'

Sayantan Kundu's hands had started to tremble. He quickly clutched them together. Maity was still looking at him with a calm expression on his face.

'And one of them is that it may not be for sale under normal circumstances.' Maity continued, 'But when it comes to the duel between the soul and the stomach, it is usually the latter that wins.'

'I . . . I couldn't help it, sir,' Sayantan almost cried out in desperation. 'If only you could see what people do in hotel rooms!'

'I have, my friend,' came Maity's calm response. 'Trust me when I tell you, I have.'

'It was easy money. Most of them never bothered to draw the curtains of their rooms. Why would they? I have walked the lane between the two buildings and looked up at the one I stay in. There are no windows anywhere. Just a rising façade of a brick wall. Nobody would even notice my tiny window.'

'Your peephole?'

'You could call it that. When I was a child, I had been to the forts of Rajasthan once. Baba had showed me how through a small hole in the walls of the forts the guards could see the enemy approaching from miles away. But the marching enemy never knew that they were being watched. "It's the same principle as in this camera, son," he would tell me, pointing to the Pentax hanging from my chest. It's called "aperture"!'

'You took photographs of the guests in those six rooms?'

'Sometimes,' Sayantan said. 'Sometimes I wouldn't. Sometimes there would be nothing to shoot. Just plain, ordinary lives of ordinary people. Smiles, tears, quarrels, dances. But at other times, some balding middle-aged office-going man would bring a prostitute in. Some bored housewife would do the same. Homosexual lovers would meet, as would straight young couples. I have seen ancient artefacts changing hands—things that clearly belong in a museum. I have seen drug deals. I have seen men and women being slapped around, threatened with knives and at gunpoint. I have seen things that you don't want to witness in your life, Mr Maity. I have seen the vile, perverse face of humanity through the lens of my camera.'

'You are a professional blackmailer, aren't you, Mr Kundu?' Maity asked, calmly.

'I am,' nodded the man. 'I shoot my photos. You can't go around blackmailing just about everyone, of course. That's how you end up dead. No, you pick and choose. Carefully. Cautiously. Usually, it is the ones who are afraid and already feeling guilty that pay. Men and women who have family. A reputation to protect. You also need to be careful in choosing the people who can *afford* to pay. No point blackmailing a young college-going couple who have come to the room straight from their tuitions. Not too rich, not too poor. Not too dangerous, not too ordinary. And if you hit the sweet spot, you get paid enough to sustain yourself for a few weeks, to take care of your cameras, to pay the rent. It's hard work. You cannot reveal who you are. They can never ever know.'

'But hang on a second!' I jumped into the conversation here. 'If you show them the photographs, won't they immediately know where you lived? Because it should be quite easy to tell from a photograph the exact spot from where it was taken.'

'Well . . .'

'And also, what is the guarantee that they won't draw the curtains in their rooms? Or not switch off the lights? What is the guarantee that you will indeed get a picture to threaten them with?'

A soft smile had appeared on the corners of Maity's lips. It gave me the impression that he knew the answers to all my questions. But he let Sayantan respond.

'There are no guarantees at all,' said the photographer. 'It's still a lousy life. But it's a better one than the one I had left behind. Sometimes, especially during sexual encounters, people would draw the curtains, sometimes they don't. I don't know much about these things, but it seems like it's a kink for them. Just like there is a voyeur in all of us, I guess there is an exhibitionist too. But you are right, when they do draw the curtains or switch off the lights, I would miss my chance there. Which is when I would shoot them when they were *not* having sex—sometimes in the rooms, but also outside the hotel, at the entrance, in the lobby, on the footpath outside the hotel. And tell them that I have pictures of them *while* having sex too.'

'You would threaten them with a lie?'

Maity's smile had broadened. Perhaps because of the incredulity in the tone of my question.

'It works, Mr Ray,' Sayantan Kundu said. 'If you choose your victim well, it works. It works because *they* know what they have done. It also works because they know that someone else does too. It works because they are afraid of what they have done and what they stand to lose.'

I sank back in my seat. I had never heard such strange things in my life.

'And to the question of their knowing where I live and where these photographs have been taken from, once again, the secret lies in choosing the right victims to blackmail, to put pressure on, to threaten, to . . . to squeeze, so to speak. I would choose those whose priority would be to save their skin, not to find out who is threatening them. In fact, I would imagine that even if I wanted to stand face to face with them, they wouldn't be able to look me in the eye. The one and only thing that they want is the assurance that if they pay me, I will get out of their lives forever. And I give them that assurance—I never fleece my victims twice. This may be a dirty game, but I have my own rules in this game too. Of course, there's a risk, and I am willing to take that risk. It will take me literally five minutes to walk out of my dingy apartment forever. Disappear. Vanish, into thin air. But hey, it pays.'

'Crime always does,' Maity now said, after a long silence. 'In the short run at least, it certainly does. But allow me to tell you what I find tragic in this . . . this story of yours. You see, you use the words "victim" and "threaten" and "fleece" without any remorse, with absolutely no thought given to the consequences of your actions. Without any consideration of how and to what extent you are changing the lives of these people you blackmail. Make no mistake, sir, you are a criminal. As many as two sections of our country's Penal Code say you are. And although your crimes may have paid so far, yet . . . here you are, sitting in front of me, almost nearing midnight, confessing to your crimes, knowing fully well that with a single phone call, I can send you to prison for the rest of your life. And I think I have a very good idea as to why you would do that, as to what led you to come and meet me.'

The young man's face had turned ghostly pale. Maity's voice was potent and grave, his look sharp and piercing, his face serious and grim.

'You saw something through that camera of yours that you shouldn't have, didn't you, Mr Kundu?'

With great difficulty, the young man somehow nodded.

'What did you see?' Maity asked.

I looked at Sayantan Kundu. His entire body had begun to tremble, so much so that he had to clutch the armrests of Maity's baroque oakwood chair to get a grip on himself. The streets outside had fallen silent. The sound of traffic had died down. Only the barks of a few strays somewhere a couple of blocks away wafted around in the night air.

'Murder, Mr Maity!' The desperate young photographer-turned-blackmailer's voice shuddered as he said those words. 'I saw a husband murder his wife!'

[2]

For several seconds, there was a heavy and distinctly uncomfortable silence in Maity's sprawling drawing room. Maity's expression was calm but serious. Sayantan Kundu had sunk back in his chair, clearly exhausted after letting the burden of his truth out. I, on the other hand, was wondering what was going on in Maity's head presently. Was he excited at the prospect of having to deal with such a bizarre set of events? Or was he disgusted by the young photographer's heinous acts? I figured it was a bit of both.

'I suppose,' Sayantan finally said, 'you would want the specifics.'

'You suppose correctly,' came Maity's response.

Sayantan took a few seconds to find the words. Then he said: 'It happened exactly a week ago. On Tuesday, the nineteenth of June. It was a hot day, but a brief spell of rain in the afternoon had cooled things down a little. A young couple had checked into one of the rooms on the third floor—the same level as I live in my own building. Seemed like a honeymoon couple. The woman was pretty, but a—how shall I say—*coarse* sort of pretty. Long straight hair. Poorly-done henna on her palm. Glass bangles. Overdone makeup. The young chap was rugged and good-looking.

It seemed to me that they . . . they weren't very well off. I mean why would they be in *that* hotel otherwise? But . . . they did seem to be in love. Deeply. They were having a good time and not just in a sexual way. They would talk for hours on end. Sometimes, I would get bored. But as you can imagine, Mr Maity, in this profession, we are not allowed to get bored. I waited for my chance. Sometimes, it seemed it would come. They would cuddle, kiss, get cosy. I'd get some good shots. But then they would break off. As if . . . as if something was stopping them, as if there was a barrier between them.'

Maity and I were listening with such rapt attention that I had not even noticed when Mahadev had come and taken the empty cups away.

'They would seem . . . sad. But then it was the woman mostly who would cheer up, throw her arms around her husband and embrace him. They would go to bed. That was when I would get the . . . the real shots.'

'From your room,' Maity said. 'Are you ever able to hear anything that happened in the rooms of that hotel? Any sound of any kind?'

'No. After I got into this . . . business, I invested in a tinted glass, had it installed on the ventilator opening. I can see everything clearly from my side of the window. But no one would be able to see me from the other side. Plus, I chose the colour of the glass in such a way that it would camouflage my window. One disadvantage of doing all this, though, was that I would hear absolutely nothing, no sound from the other side.'

'I see,' nodded Maity. 'Interesting, very interesting!'

'Anyway, I got some really good shots of the couple. In . . . in the act, you know? Shots that would suffice for my purpose. The best shots are the ones that show the faces clearly. I'm sorry you are having to hear all these details, but . . .'

'As despicable as your crimes are, Mr Kundu,' Maity interrupted, 'I'm afraid the details are important. That's usually where the devil resides.'

'I understand,' Sayantan nodded. 'Like I said, I got some good shots. But that night, while they were in the . . . you know . . . the height of their act, something else caught my attention through the lens. At first, it seemed quite funny to me. In fact, I remember having chuckled behind my camera. The room exactly below them was occupied by a middle-aged couple. Perhaps in their late forties or early fifties. They had checked in a day before, on the eighteenth. When the younger couple were having sex, I could see the middle-aged couple look up at the ceiling of their room. They could obviously hear the noises coming from the room above. And they were clearly not amused. The wife said something to the husband, the husband replied angrily. There was a brief quarrel between the two. It was amusing, to be honest . . . this . . . this contrast between what was going on in those two rooms. One on top of the other.'

'What happened then?'

'The quarrel stopped after some time. The woman went to bed, held a pillow over her ear. That didn't seem to work, because she flung the pillow across the room, and it almost hit her husband. The husband yelled at her—she yelled back. That's when the real quarrel started. It all came to blows. The wife seemed furious.'

'And this young couple in the room above . . .' Maity interjected with a suggestion of a question.

'Yes,' nodded Sayantan, 'they had . . . finished by then. They were exhausted. The couple below were now in a bitter fight. The woman had started slapping her husband left, right and centre. She was screaming and sobbing. The husband was taking all the hits. But after a while, he punched his wife right across the face. Sent her flying across the room and on to the bed.'

'He . . . he killed her?' I asked, apprehensively.

'No,' Sayantan sighed. 'The punch was hard. A boxer's punch. But it didn't kill her. Knocked the wits out of her all right. She kept sobbing and trembling. I zoomed in to find that her lips had swollen up and were bleeding. The husband walked out of the room, slamming the door shut behind him. By this time, even the couple on the top floor had heard the squabble downstairs. The woman seemed concerned. The young husband came to the window, even opened it. Probably to see if he could hear what was going on. He gave up. Shut the window and went back to his wife. Tried to comfort her. The wife put on some clothes, rushed to the bathroom and returned immediately with a glass in her hand. She placed the glass upside down on the floor of the room and then placed her ear on the other side of the glass. The husband said something; she put her finger on her lips and shushed him. Then she signalled him to come and join her. The husband knelt on the floor and put his ear to the glass. It seemed he too heard the woman below sobbing. They took turns to listen and seemed to say something to each other.'

'And where was the man when all of this was happening? The man in the room below, I mean?'

'He wasn't in the room. I'm not quite sure where he was, because the front façade of the hotel isn't visible from my room.'

'I see. Please continue.'

'The middle-aged woman had calmed down by now. Pulled out a handkerchief from her purse and dabbed at her lips. The kerchief turned red. There was something embroidered in the corner of the kerchief . . . some letters of some sort. I quickly changed my lens to get a proper view.'

'Did you get the name?' I asked, expectantly.

Sayantan Kundu looked at me and said, 'I did! It was Edith.'

'Edith?' I asked. 'Just Edith? No surname?'

'People don't embroider their full names on their handkerchiefs, Prakash,' Maity said.

I realized the stupidity of my question and Maity turned his attention back to Sayantan Kundu.

'She was still bleeding; it was a nasty punch. The kerchief was completely red, but she was still dabbing her lips with it and staring blankly into the void. I quickly got a few shots of her. It was a sad, sad face. I was sure she would get a black eye in the morning. But . . .'

There was a brief pause in Sayantan's narration but it seemed like an eternity. The late-night breeze was rustling the sheers of Maity's drawing room windows. The delicate fragrance of the jasmines from Maity's garden below was filling the room with a strange mood of intoxication. Even the street dogs had stopped barking. I couldn't bear the suspense any more.'

'But what?' I asked.

'The morning never came for her!'

Yet again, a long pause. Sayantan Kundu had hung his head. Maity's famous frown had appeared on his forehead.

'The young couple went back to bed,' Sayantan muttered. 'The woman downstairs too must have cried herself to sleep. I was up though, looking through my camera. Boredom is not a luxury I can afford. And . . . and not only that . . . I don't know why . . . I can't explain it in words . . . it seemed to me that something would happen that night. Call it a foreboding, or a paparazzo's instinct. Something was just not right. I couldn't place my finger on it and tell you exactly what it was. But there was something . . . odd. So I didn't take my chances. Sat there all night, with my eyes on the lens. The couple on the top had fallen fast asleep in each other's arms. The woman downstairs had fallen asleep too. The bell from the Assembly of God Church nearby had just struck two gongs. My eyes were tired. I wanted to shut them, even if for a minute. But I couldn't. I just couldn't. It seemed to me that if I did, I would miss something. Something . . . something important, something ominous, something . . . diabolic. And I was right. A few minutes after the second gong, the door to the room downstairs opened slowly. Whoever opened it didn't enter right away, stood in the doorway for a while. I could see the heavy boots and part of the legs. Then he came in and locked the door behind him. It was the husband of the woman sleeping on the bed.'

I found myself sitting on the edge of my seat. Maity was unfazed.

'He stood by the edge of the bed, looking down at his sleeping wife for the longest time. Who knows how long, could be five, ten minutes. I . . . I didn't think he meant to do it. But then something came over him. You know that moment when you are standing at the edge of a great drop, perhaps the terrace of a skyscraper, or the ledge over a high cliff? And you are in two minds. Should you jump? Or should you walk away? You know that moment I'm talking about, don't you, Mr Maity?'

Maity nodded silently.

'I don't know . . . I don't think the people who do jump truly realize what they are doing. Perhaps the realization dawns upon them *after* they have taken that single step forward. Or perhaps it doesn't. But it doesn't matter. Because by then, it's too late. There's no coming back from there.'

Sayantan Kundu looked up and stared directly at Maity. Tears were rolling down his eyes, and his voice was shaking. I felt bad for the young man, despite all the vile acts he had committed.

'He killed her, Mr Maity,' Sayantan whispered. 'Grabbed a pillow and held it on her face, even as she woke up and realized what was happening. Smothered her, choked her, suffocated the last bubble of air out of her lungs till her limbs stopped swinging wildly and she gently withered away. It was . . . it was the ghastliest sight I have ever seen. But somehow—and I am both ashamed and frightened to tell you this—I just could not take my eyes off my camera. I just couldn't look away. Because there was an aesthetic to it. The aesthetic of death. Like you see in one of those Renaissance paintings. Life in one frame, and the absence of it in another. Barely a few moments apart. It was as if I had seen a . . . a work of art. A beautiful photograph. Perhaps the most beautiful photograph I had ever seen. Either outside, or through the lens of my camera.'

Having said this much, the young man fell silent. He hung his head and pinched his eyes with his thumb and his forefinger, as if a great agony was trilling through his brains and destroying him from the insides of his very being. Maity was silent for almost a minute, thinking, his eyes fixed on the floor right in front of him. Then he looked up at Sayantan Kundu and said, 'What do you want from me?'

The response didn't come at once. After much hesitation, the young man said, 'The last week has been terrible for me, Mr Maity. I'm not a voyeur or an extortionist by choice. I turned to it only for the money, to survive. I hate every moment of this . . . this life. The burden of conscience, the fear of being caught, the guilt. I tell myself that I have rules. But deep down, I know what I am doing is fundamentally wrong. But then, you were right about that duel. When hunger comes knocking, all values and ethics go flying out of that tiny window of my room. And then, like every other person in this world who hates his job but still goes to work every morning, I go and sit behind that camera too. But *this*? No, this is different. This is too heavy a burden on my soul, or whatever is left of it, whatever I haven't sold yet.'

'You haven't answered my question, Mr Kundu,' Maity said, his voice devoid of empathy.

Sayantan Kundu took a deep breath and sat up straight in his chair. Then he unzipped his satchel and pulled out a large envelope, extended it towards Maity and said: 'That man needs to be caught and punished for what he has done, Mr Maity. I have heard great things about you. Word on the street is that you can do what no one else can, not even the police. And for obvious reasons, I cannot go to the police with this. In this envelope are the photographs of the entire act. The faces of both the killer and the victim are clearly visible. We also seem to have the victim's name, at least her first name. Those are good starting points, in my opinion. I want you to . . .'

Sayantan Kundu paused abruptly, then picked up his flow again.

'I request you to find the killer. And I request you to bring him to justice. I . . . I know these are big words coming from someone like me, someone who has done the things that I have. But trust me when I tell you this, I'm done. I'm never going to do this again, even if I starve to death. I'll lift crates, drive a cab, work in a grocery store, but I will never peep into people's lives ever again. That is my promise to you.'

I looked at Maity. His hawk eyes hadn't moved an inch from the young man's face. And it continued to stay there. Then, very slowly, the following words came out of Janardan Maity's mouth:

'The pleasure of voyeurism is a dangerous thing, Mr Kundu. As are the aesthetics of violence that you spoke about a few minutes ago. Unknown to man, these are some of the most potent narcotics that a fragmented mind can consume and succumb to. They give you a delusion of power over the people you are spying on. They also trigger that part of our brains that was dominant when we humans used to be nothing but killer apes. There is a certain lust involved in witnessing a violent scene. Like any other intoxication gone too far, it might make you throw up later, make you feel guilty about it, make you promise never to do it again, but don't forget that *while* the murder was being committed, you couldn't take your eyes off the lens of your camera. You couldn't stop.'

Sayantan Kundu pulled back his extended hand and hung his head.

'Long ago,' Maity wasn't finished, 'I used to know a man who had a peculiar habit. He liked to ram his speeding car into trees and poles and walls. Deliberately! Sounds strange, doesn't it? He had broken every possible bone in his body, suffered dozens of concussions, had almost died on several occasions, even lost an eye. He wasn't suicidal, in the conventional sense of the term. One day, when he was in his hospital bed, all messed up, almost an inch away from death, I asked him: Why do you do this? And he gave me the strangest answer that I have ever heard. He said: Because I like it! And because I can't stop myself from doing it!'

Sayantan Kundu listened to Maity in silence. Maity, in turn, stared back at him and took his time to utter his next few words.

'So you see, Mr Kundu, when you sit in that chair of mine, and try to assure me that you are never going to do it again, I must also tell you in return that I have my doubts. Because by now, you are addicted to it. By now, it's not about the money any more. The money is just incidental. As long as you have a camera, and dare I say, even without it, you will continue to peer into people's private lives. I feel bad for you. Because you clearly don't want to. But you will, no matter how hard you try, no matter how many crates you lift and how honest a life you live, you still will. It's a curse you can't walk away from as easily as you are making it sound.'

'I . . . I can at least try,' Sayantan Kundu whispered. 'Can't I?'

Maity nodded, and rose to his feet. 'That you can. That is one thing that we all can—try. I, at my end, will try to ensure

that this man, this killer, is found, caught and punished for
the crime he has committed. You can leave the envelope on
the table in front of you, I will take a look at its contents
tomorrow morning. Because the clock is about to strike
midnight, and till I met you and heard your story, I was under
the impression that this night couldn't get any worse. So, if
you will excuse me, Prakash and I would like to have our
dinner. My servant is loyal, but old. And I wouldn't like to
keep him up any more than I have to. Goodnight!'

[3]

The next morning, I woke up in Maity's guest bedroom, the one I usually crash in when I am staying over, and just as the memories of the previous night's bizarre incidents had started flooding in, Mahadev brought me my morning tea and said, 'Dadababu has stepped out for a bit, he said he will come back by eight.'

'Did he tell you where he was going?' I asked.

'No, that he didn't,' Mahadev grumbled as he turned towards the door. 'Does he ever say anything to me any more? More than fifty years I have been in this house, nursed him like a baby. Now he's all grown up. Comes and goes as he likes. Doesn't have his food on time, doesn't even sleep properly. That's what happens when you deal with those lunatics and murderers all day long . . .'

As Mahadev's voice faded out behind the closed door, a fond smile crept on to my lips. As I took a contented sip on the fresh brew of tea (which Maity bought from yet another unknown source), I couldn't help but wonder how even such a great detective and such an enlightened mind—the scourge of dangerous criminals and vile minds—had someone to scold and reprimand him from time to time.

The morning light was streaming in over the beautifully embroidered curtains of the window, and the mercury had still not begun to rise. My mind went back to last night's unexpected guest. Maity was clearly disappointed by everything Sayantan Kundu had done, but it was also true that his crimes were nothing compared to the other, much more serious crime that he had witnessed and had the moral courage to bring to Maity's notice. Knowing my dear friend for so many years now, I knew that if nothing else, Maity would appreciate that courage and would take on the case based on that merit alone. I also knew him well enough to predict that he was not the sort of person to not do anything about a murder, whether or not there was clear evidence of the crime—photographic, in this case.

Which was exactly why another thought crept into my mind. Wasn't the case too simple for someone like Maity? I knew Maity only liked baffling puzzles. But here, the face of the perpetrator, the face of the victim—both were known to us. Where was the challenge then? All he had to do was to find out who the killer was, where he lived and that would be the end of it. Of course, the killer may have fled, but knowing Maity's contacts with the police network of the city and beyond, it wouldn't be too difficult for him to trace the man, would it? Another problem that he might have to face would be to hide the identity of the man who took those photographs, but even I, sitting in this room with my morning cup of tea, could think of several solutions to that problem.

Why did Maity take on the case then? It was quite unlike him to get involved in a problem that did not test his intelligence enough, that did not challenge him. What had he seen in the case that I had not? What was, as they say, the catch?

As all these thoughts were going through my mind, I suddenly noticed the yellow envelope on the writing desk at the far end of the room—the envelope that Sayantan had left last night. I quickly kept my cup aside, jumped out of bed and snatched the envelope from the desk, returning to the bed and pulling out the contents as I did.

The first thing to come out of the envelope was a sheet of paper with two different addresses on it. The first was that of a building on Park Lane, so I assumed it was where Sayantan lived. The other was that of Hotel Fairy Glen, also on Park Lane. From the numbers of the two buildings, it seemed as if they were located adjacent to each other: 16 and 18/1.

Then out came a bunch of photographs. With nervous and yet excited hands, I browsed through them. They were all of the room in which the murder had happened. The scene of the crime. Frame by frame, I saw everything that Sayantan had described last night. His descriptions had been more or less accurate, so I won't repeat them here. Except to focus attention on the two subjects of his photographs. The wife did seem like she was in her early fifties. Frail, colourless, devoid of any joy or smile. The angle was a bit off, but she seemed like she was of a short height, perhaps barely a tad over five feet or so. In the early photographs, she seemed haggard and frustrated, with a look of abject sorrow pasted on her pale face—the ideal image of an exhausted wife, defeated in the battle of life and domesticity, with no outlet to vent her frustrations. The husband, on whom she did seem to take out her frustrations in the subsequent photographs, was a burly man of roughly the same age as his wife.

He wore glasses, had a receding hairline and a paunch, and was at least 6 feet tall, if not more. The woman was dressed in a flimsy crimson nightgown all throughout, and the husband was dressed in a pair of black pants and a vest in the early photographs, and a white shirt added on top of that in the latter ones. The woman wore a cross on a slender gold chain around her neck, and the man had a hat kept on the table near the reading lamp, although he wasn't seen wearing it even once in the photographs.

Curiously enough, the photographs from the room on the top—where the honeymoon couple were staying—were missing from the bunch. I figured Sayantan had decided to give us only the images from the scene of the crime.

I did notice the handkerchief though, with the lady's name embroidered in green in one corner. From the way it was covered in blood, it was quite evident that the cut on her lips had been a deep one. On careful observation, I noticed a few drops of blood on the pillow cover as well, the one on which she had cried herself to sleep.

'Shouldn't have drunk coffee so late in the night!'

I was so lost in the photographs that Maity's words startled me. He entered the room, flung his sling bag aside and poured himself a glass of water from the jug on the nightstand.

'Couldn't get a wink of sleep,' he said. 'Old age is catching up with me, Prakash.'

'Where have you been?' I asked.

Maity gulped down the water, placed the glass back on the nightstand and said, 'Just needed some fresh air. I see you've gone through the photographs?'

'Yes, I have.'

'Kid's got talent. Pity he had to resort to such questionable acts. Could have made a name for himself, with a bit of luck and perhaps a little push.'

'He didn't give us the photos of the top room though.'

'Oh no, he did,' Maity picked up the sling bag from the table and pulled a bunch of photos out.

'Oh!' I exclaimed. 'He did? Where had you taken them, then?'

Maity gave me the photos and said after a brief pause, 'As I said, I needed a bit of fresh air, wanted to take a closer look at them.'

I frowned, then smiled as I looked at my dear friend, whom I always knew as a serious, knowledgeable and enlightened man of impeccable ethics and values—to the extent of being nearly self-admittedly old-fashioned. A hermit of sorts. Somehow, I couldn't imagine Janardan Maity leering at photographs of a young married couple having sex! Which is why his next words seemed all the more surprising to me.

'They were . . .' he muttered under his breath, 'they were so erotic!'

Maity continued to stare blankly out of the window for a few seconds. Then, as if a trance was broken, he looked at the photographs in my hands and stepped out of the room. I took a few moments to try and understand what was going on. Why had Maity taken only those specific photographs out to study? Instead of focusing on the scene of the crime— the room where the murder had taken place? I looked at the photographs, and he was right. The passionate young couple were involved in various acts of erotic lovemaking. The kind we see in the movies. It is said that one mustn't lie to one's readers, so I must embarrassingly admit that

I was just about beginning to enjoy looking through the photographs, when a resounding yell of 'Breakfast' echoed through the mansion and made me hurriedly shove all the photographs back into the envelope and get out of bed. But before I had done so, I had had enough time to notice that both the young man and the woman were quite good-looking, although—as our photographer friend's keen eyes had astutely observed—they did seem to come from a slightly unrefined layer of society. The hairstyle, the attire, the guy's earrings, the woman's tacky dye, the cheap shoes—everything fit the description that Sayantan Kundu had given us last night.

After a quick breakfast, Maity and I stepped out. I had expected our first stop would be either at the hotel or at our Peeping Tom's cabin. But Maity seemed to have other plans. He asked the cab to stop at a photography store on a quiet tree-lined lane near Rawdon Street and stepped inside with me in tow.

'Excuse me,' he addressed the aged Parsi owner of the shop, 'can you tell me if this photo paper was purchased from your store?'

I looked down at the photograph that Maity had shown the gentleman. It was of the middle-aged couple. The wife was standing in front of the open wardrobe with a glum face and either putting something in or bringing something out. The man was sitting on the bed speaking on his cell phone. This was one of the early photographs, before all the chaos ensued.

The old Parsi gentleman paused an old Hollywood Western he was watching on a small television set, took a casual look at the photograph and said briefly, 'Yes.'

'I figured,' Maity smiled.

'Of course you figured!' the man said in a gruff voice, as he opened a stainless-steel snuff box and snorted a pinch. 'The store's name is stamped on the envelope!'

Maity winked at me and addressed the gentleman again, 'But I am assuming these were not developed here, were they?'

'No,' the man said as he proceeded to resume his movie. 'Would have remembered.'

'Could you by chance remember the customer who had purchased this paper from you?'

The elderly man's forefinger stopped over the button of his remote, as his head slowly turned towards Maity, 'Who wants to know?'

I looked at the gentleman. His face was lined with age and wisdom; there was a look of caution and distrust in his eyes and he looked like the sort of man whom no one ought to take for granted. I looked down at his hands—they looked extremely rough. Maity later told me that people who develop photographs often had rough fingers and palms, thanks to the corrosive chemicals they had to handle.

Maity smiled briefly to diffuse the tension in the air and said in a soft voice, 'I chanced upon this photograph at a friend's place; he is an art director. Said some freelancer had left him his portfolio, wanted to get a gig. A remarkable photograph, wouldn't you agree? Not exactly Cartier-Bresson, but whoever's taken this shot has a keen eye—you've got to give that to him.'

'Or her!' I quickly added.

The man placed the remote on the glass surface of the shop's counter and looked at me.

Maity continued calmly, 'I was wondering if I could get a name, or perhaps an address, or even a description, I would love to work with him.'

'Or her?' the man said.

Maity nodded with a gentle smile.

'Kid's got a keen eye, yes,' the man continued, staring directly at Maity, 'but so do I. I've been in this business for over sixty years now, mister. That's more than the number of years that you or this young whippersnapper pal of yours has been on this planet. And from experience, I can tell you that the greatest camera ever invented is the human eye, and you take that from a man who knows. Who's been around. Who has seen it all. And who can see as easily when he is being taken advantage of. When he is being lied to.'

Maity pursed his lips and nodded respectfully.

'I have offended you, sir,' he said. 'And I apologize. I am looking for the man who took this photograph. It's a serious matter—a matter of life and death, in fact. And I can respectfully assure you that no harm is going to come upon this man, should you choose to divulge this information. If you choose not to, I would understand and accept your decision.'

The man took another sniff of snuff from his box, rubbed his nose with his knuckles and said: 'Now, wasn't that easier? This current generation! No ethics, no respect. Overconfidence and arrogance in the name of assertion. Always looking for shortcuts.'

More than two-thirds of those words were uttered while the man was staring directly at me, so I was wondering how to react. But before I got a chance to say or do anything, the gentleman said: 'I don't usually divulge information about my customers. Bad for business. But it's a matter of life and death, you say. And you say it like you mean it—that much these old hawk eyes can tell. Don't know the name. Young Bong chap. Has been coming to my store for several years now, five or six at least. Carries a couple of Canons around. Doesn't believe in all that digital crap. Buys film from me. Now *that's* respect. And that's not for sale.'

'Unkempt, untidy hair?' Maity asked. 'Broad face? Thin moustache? Mole on the tip of right ear?'

'That's the one. Used to buy the regular stuff right over there on that shelf behind you. Of late, has been insisting on buying premium film. Must have got a gig somewhere.'

I had not seen any mole on Sayantan's entire face, let alone the tip of his right ear. Maity had. Despite the fact that he was sitting on the young man's left and I on his right.

Maity thanked the Parsi gentleman profusely and turned around. Before we stepped out of his store, before we sat in the cab, and before the sound of a Texan gunfight filled the inside of the store again, a few more words, spoken in the same gruff voice reached our ears: 'Wouldn't go too far with that kind of hair though. Hair matters. Changes your portrait. Entirely! And if there's one person who ought to know at least that much, it's a photographer!'

[4]

'What was that all about?' I asked Maity, as our cab started off towards Park Street.

'A stranger comes to you, admits to a questionable addiction, shows you a bunch of photographs and claims that he saw something as serious as murder,' Maity whispered. 'You ought to check him out, see if he can be trusted.'

The thought hadn't occurred to me. I said, 'You think he could be lying about the whole thing?'

'The whole thing, part of it, none of it. There's only one way to know—paying him a visit and peeping through that hole in his wall.'

Park Lane was a busy and congested lane just off Park Street, on the other side of St Xavier's College. On Maity's instruction, our cab turned right into Rafi Ahmed Kidwai Road from Park Street, and then right again from the corner of Bhikharam Chandmal to enter an ocean of black heads bobbing up and down, on seeing which, our driver threw his hands up in the air and suggested that we walk the rest of the distance.

'Good man!' Maity tipped the driver generously and stepped out of the car. I joined him on the road, as our cab slowly backed out of the lane and disappeared from view.

Hundreds of shops and buildings lined both the pavements. Litter strewn across the asphalt. Rainwater flowing into sewers on both sides of the lane. Not a very presentable part of the city. But Maity sniffed in the atmosphere with a happy smile on his face and said, 'Ah! Kolkata!'

We started walking towards the east, towards Mullickbazar. Hundreds of people swarming the lane, rushing past us in both directions, avoiding collisions. Two-wheelers honking every now and then. A little girl running around with a tea kettle and five earthen pots in her hand. Trading in full swing. Street-food vendors tossing chow mein and chopping impossibly red watermelons. All in all, the unmistakable buzz of a busy commercial road in one of the most cosmopolitan cities in the country.

'Had come here many years ago,' said Maity, as he looked around with a smile on his face.

'For a case?' I asked.

'No, no, no, you and your cases!' The irritation in his voice and on his face was unmistakable. 'To buy a Svengali deck. Can't see the shop any more though.'

'What deck?'

Maity had started muttering under his breath by now, 'Eight, ten, there's twelve, and fourteen, ah . . . there it is . . .'

Rising before us into a grim, grey and overcast sky was an imposing building clearly built during the days of the Raj. The front façade bore enough evidence of that fact. It was also evident to us from the façade that the building had seen better days. Much, much better days. It was in an abject state of decay, and I have never seen Maity's mood change so quickly. His wide grin disappeared in an instant on seeing the building. He made a clicking sound with his tongue expressing regret and lament, and before he could spiral down into one of his notoriously foul moods again, I quickly asked, 'This is the building where Sayantan lives, isn't it?'

'Yes,' he said briefly, his eyes still stuck on the tragedy painted on the gloomy canvas of the sky. The original colour of the paint on the building was now impossible to decipher. Almost half of it was covered in soot, the other half in moss. A bunch of weeds had crept their way up and—believe it or not—*into* the walls of the building. Red bricks were jutting out from here and there, revealing the ugly skeleton underneath the uglier flesh. The windows that looked down on us must have been beautifully decorated in the days of yore, but now, torn petticoats, patched shirts and other frayed items of clothing hung from them. There was a distinct signature of arrogant neglect all over the building.

'Come,' said Maity, as we walked into the building through the front entrance that no one had bothered to shut or guard. There were dozens of letterboxes on the walls right inside the entrance, and by the looks of the dense cobwebs on them, it seemed to us that they hadn't been opened for years now. As we walked past the graveyard of those mailboxes, we were faced by an ancient elevator that looked like it was still in the process of being dug out of an archaeological site.

'Nope!'

Maity uttered that single word looking at the elevator and proceeded towards the stairs on the left. I hurriedly and happily joined him.

'The Svengali deck is a deck of cards,' Maity said, as we started making our way to the third floor where Sayantan lived, 'slightly modified to perform magic tricks with. To the naked eye, it would seem just like any other normal deck of cards, but it isn't exactly so. The Svengali deck is one of many trick decks in the world of magic.'

I had no idea that Janardan Maity was interested in the subject of magic too. I knew he was a voracious reader and that he read about anything and everything under the sun, but that he took such an active interest in magic tricks—so much so that he had come all the way here to purchase a prop, presumably to practise with it—that information was new to me. He hadn't told me this even during the show we had gone to watch the previous night. The thought once again occurred to me that the man would always remain a mystery to me, and I could now understand why he was in such a bad mood last night.

'How exactly is this deck modified?' I asked.

'I'm not supposed to talk about it,' he winked at me. 'Magician's code. Only two magicians can speak of such things to each other.'

Before I could say anything further, Maity had reached and stopped before a particular door in, what can be best described as, a hellhole of a corridor. There were stains and stench everywhere, mostly of paan, urine and marijuana. The two lights flickering at the end of the corridor were so far away, and covered with so much soot, that it took me quite a few seconds to realize that they were, in fact, one single tube light and not two separate bulbs. The rest of the corridor was near dark, and I was quite apprehensive of what invisible sticky floor I was stepping on. Midway, my blind step knocked away an empty bottle lying bang in the middle of the corridor, shocking the living daylights out of me. One thing was for sure, and I only realized it after I had entered the building—that it was quite a large one. It hadn't seemed so from the road downstairs. It gave me the creeps, to be honest. Maity seemed unfazed though, and in a calm, composed and business-like manner, he knocked on Sayantan Kundu's door.

'Ah, Mr Maity,' said Sayantan Kundu, as the door opened a crack. 'Please, please come in.'

'Prakash is right behind me too,' said Maity, 'eager to step in.'

'Of course, of course, Mr Ray! Please come. Thank you so much for coming. You will please excuse the mess.' With a look of embarrassment on his face, Sayantan Kundu had gotten busy in making the impossible effort to solve the problem of disarray in his den, when Maity stopped him and assured him that we were fine, we didn't need to sit down or be comfortable, and that he would rather be shown the window in question as soon as possible.

I would not waste any time describing the little nest that our photographer friend had set up for himself, except to merely say that I couldn't imagine how someone could live in so filthy and such untidy an environment. Instead, I forced my attention to turn towards a small rectangle on one of the walls of the room. It was a tiny ventilator all right. Normally, ventilators are built higher up on the walls, closer to the ceiling. For reasons unknown to me—and to Maity as well, I asked him later—this one was built around five-odd feet above the floor. Therefore, a man of Sayantan's height would have to bend down to peep through it, and if he were to sit on a normal chair, the hole would be too high for his eyes to reach. Which probably explained the presence of the two thick cushions on the chair placed next to the wall. There was also a camera—an old-fashioned Canon—placed on a tripod in front of the chair. Also placed next to the chair was a small round table, and what seemed like a wooden footstool. On two low shelves that were reachable from the chair itself were kept two more cameras, quite a few lenses, boxes of Fuji film and various other stuff which I presume were related to photography, including the patched leatherette satchel that I had seen him carry last night.

Maity pointed to a door on the left and said, 'I'm presuming your bathroom doubles up as your darkroom?'

'Yes,' Sayantan smiled, 'I started developing my photographs myself, after I . . .'

He trailed off. I looked at Maity, who was still looking around the room with his keen, searching eyes. If the Parsi gentleman was right, then I knew that the two cameras on Maity's face were clicking hundreds and thousands of photographs of that tiny room, neatly saving the images in the vault of his brain, only to be accessed at some later point in time.

'May I?' Maity asked inquiringly, pointing at the Canon on the tripod.

On Sayantan's nod, Maity gently approached the chair and stared at the cushion, the position of the chair, the camera itself, and the gap between the chair and the wall for almost three minutes. All without touching or disturbing a single thing. He then bent down to look into the peephole, and then took a closer look at the camera itself, examining it for quite some time.

Then he straightened his back up, looked down at the cushion and said, 'You seem to spend a significant amount of time at this camera.'

'Yes,' said Sayantan, 'it's all I do now.'

'Don't you go out at all?'

'Only to a café downstairs,' said the young man. 'Once in a while.'

I cast a sideways glance at an unclean, overused and soot-covered kerosene stove in one of the alcoves at the far end of the room. There were a few potatoes lying around in one corner and a couple of small glass jars next to them, with various spices inside. A small saucepan and a few other utensils lay here and there, in a manner that fit the overall vibe of the room.

Maity gently pulled the chair back a little by its backrest, inserted himself in the space he had freed up and sat down, pulling the chair back under him towards the camera, adjusting his position so as to allow him to place his eye on the viewfinder.

For the next ten minutes or so, Janardan Maity seemed to completely forget about the presence of two other souls in the room. Sayantan was a photographer by profession, and by his own admission, patience was a virtue that was necessary for his job. So he may have been used to it. But the entire thing became so intolerable for me that I started feeling restless. So much so, that I tried drawing Maity's attention by clearing my throat, coughing, tapping my shoes on the floor and deliberately making other noises, but nothing worked. It was as if Maity was lost in his own world.

'I have only one chair,' Sayantan finally said to me, noticing that I had reached the end of my patience, 'but please feel free to sit on the bed.'

'When did he check out?'

Before I could say no-thank-you to the young man, Maity's voice rung out from behind the camera.

'That very night,' Sayantan replied. 'After the murder, he sat in silence by the edge of the bed for a few seconds. As if in a trance, his head buried in his hands. Then he suddenly seemed to come to his senses. He shot up from his seat and came to the window. Looked out of it here and there. I'm assuming all he could see was the brick wall of this building. As I had told you before, there are no windows on the side of my building.'

'Except yours,' Maity's eyes were still fixed on the viewfinder, his right hand resting lightly on the camera.

'Except mine,' agreed Sayantan, 'and he did look at mine. For a long time, he did. Almost a minute, or probably two.'

'What was your reaction then?'

'I knew that he would be able to see only the glass, if that. The glass is tinted on the outside. He couldn't possibly have seen *me*.'

'But you were afraid?'

Sayantan Kundu did not respond. Maity slowly turned his head around and looked at his face.

'I was,' Sayantan nodded. 'I have to admit, I was. I had never seen anything like that before. A slap or a punch here and there, that's all that I had seen so far. But this was different. A woman's life had been taken. Yes, I was afraid.'

I looked at Maity. He had turned his head back to the camera, but had not placed his eye on it yet. It seemed to me he was thinking.

'Can I ask you something, Mr Kundu?'

'Sure, sir.'

'Have you ever seen death before?'

'Excuse me?'

'Death, Mr Kundu!' Maity asked again. 'Have you seen anyone die right in front of your eyes?'

'My father, yes. He died of cancer—pancreas. He was cured once, we spent almost all our money on his treatment. But then there was a relapse. It took him away this time, didn't even give him a fighting chance. Then my mother, just a few months later. She had a heart attack.'

'I see.'

'You think that's what scared me?' Sayantan's voice shook a little, sounding hurt and unsure of what Maity's question was trying to imply. 'A violent death? A murder? A crime of passion?'

'Speaking of passion,' Maity's voice was calm in the face of Sayantan Kundu's emotions, his eyes once again fixed on the camera. 'When did the other couple check out? The passionate one?'

'The next morning.'

'The very next morning?' Maity stood up from the chair and came around to where we were standing.

'Yes,' said Sayantan, 'check-out time is 10 a.m.; they checked out around half an hour before that.'

'I can see that both rooms seem to be vacant now. Prakash, have a look. Has anyone checked into those two rooms over the last one week? Ever since the night of the murder?'

'Yes, there was a family of three who checked into the room below. Father, mother, little girl. They checked out after a couple of nights.'

'And in the top room?'

'No, that room has been vacant ever since.'

As I sat down at the chair and placed my eye on the viewfinder, a familiar image of a room emerged in front of my eyes. I had seen the room in the photographs: this is where the poor woman had been smothered to death. With unaccustomed hands, I slightly adjusted the camera upwards to look at the top room. This room seemed familiar too. This is where the younger couple had stayed. Both rooms were dark now, only partially visible in the dim daylight streaming in through the windows.

'That's natural,' Maity's voice came floating across the room. 'Most hotels have a specific room that they like to give out to honeymooners.'

'If you look carefully,' said Sayantan, 'the honeymooners' room is slightly bigger too. Not much, but just a tad.'

'Really?' I remarked.

'I did notice that,' said Maity. 'Probably on account of a bigger bathroom. I wouldn't be surprised if there's a bathtub in there.'

I tried to take a closer look, but couldn't figure out what either Maity or Sayantan were saying. Both the rooms looked exactly the same to me in terms of size. I suddenly remembered that Sayantan had said that he had the view of six rooms from his peephole. I tried turning the camera around to find the other four. And as I did, two things happened. First, for several seconds, all I could see was a brick wall. I realized the lens had been zoomed a little too much, and I didn't want to disturb it so I just kept searching for the other four rooms.

Second, I heard a peculiar question being asked by Maity to Sayantan: 'Mr Kundu, a few minutes ago, you said that when he looked out of his window after killing his wife in a fit of rage, all that the killer could have probably seen from his room was the tinted glass of your ventilator, and you went on to add: *if that*. I'm curious, what exactly did you mean by those two words?'

'Well, for one, it was night-time. My window is quite small, as you can see. The distance between the two buildings is significant, although it may not seem that way. I was looking at him through the camera, I can zoom in. He was looking at my window with his naked eyes.'

'And I suppose your room was dark? Your lights were switched off?'

'Always.'

'And his weren't?'

Sayantan thought for a few seconds and said, 'Not at that moment when he was looking out, no. But then he pulled the curtains and switched off the lights.'

'I see!' said Maity. 'Very interesting! What did you do then?'

'I . . . I waited. Trying to catch a glimpse of what was going on inside the room. The curtains are more of sheers, not blinds. But as I said, it was a cloudy night, quite dark outside, so I couldn't see anything. A few minutes later, I saw the man leave the room.'

'Hang on a second. How did you know the man left the room? The curtains were drawn, right?'

'Yes, but when the man opened the door, a thin triangular beam of light came into the room from the corridor outside and lit up the curtain. Then it disappeared instantly. I could draw only one conclusion from that fact.'

'It didn't occur to you that someone may have come *into* the room? Instead of the man leaving the room?'

'No, that's not possible.'

'*Not possible?*' cried Maity. 'You seem remarkably sure of that claim.'

'Why would someone come into the room where a man had murdered his wife? That too at half past two in the night?'

'Oh, I can give you several reasons why. The man was talking on his cell phone earlier—we have seen that in one of the photographs. I wonder whom he was talking to. A close friend? A lover? Someone whom he could confide in and tell what he had done in a fit of rage? Someone who could have come to help him, console him? And the most important reason of all. What happened to the body? How did it leave the room? Did it vanish into thin air? Because I don't suppose the late Mrs Edith's husband just carried his wife's corpse past the receptionist in the lobby, did he?'

'That's exactly what he did!'

I turned around from the camera to find even Maity stunned and frowning at the young photographer's outrageous claim. Sayantan Kundu walked over to a shelf over his bed and pulled out another bunch of photographs. He then flipped through them, pulled a few of them out and slammed them on the round table. Both Maity and I rushed to them in an instant.

'There are some photographs of that room down there that I hadn't left with you in the envelope last night. Didn't think they might be useful—to be honest. But I suspect that you are trying to establish if what I saw was indeed what I thought had happened. Well, there you are. Look for yourself!'

Maity and I looked at the photographs together. Many months after the story was over, when Maity and I would sit back in his drawing room and talk about this bizarre case, he would often say that those specific photographs were some of the most extraordinary aspects of this truly mystifying and mind-baffling puzzle. And I, for one, entirely agreed with him.

In the first photograph, the curtains on the windows of the room where the murder happened were drawn and the room was dark. In the second, the curtains were still drawn, but the light inside the room had been switched on. Since the light was at the far end of the room on the writing desk and the husband was between the light and the curtain, his silhouette could be seen on the curtain, which acted as a screen.

'Remarkable!' I heard Maity whisper. Even under such tense circumstances, I could not help but wonder how talented a photographer Sayantan Kundu was.

By now, we had seen enough pictures of the husband to know that the silhouette was his. The tall, burly figure, the glasses, the paunch, the receding curly hairline—everything was visible in the silhouette that had appeared on the sheers.

In the third photograph, he could be seen in the act of propping up what can only be presumed was his wife's lifeless body against the headboard of the bed. Her head was tilted forward, and it seemed that even the strong man was struggling to carry his wife's body. Maity had once told me that dead weight was a dangerous thing, and almost impossible to fathom unless witnessed first-hand.

In the next photograph, the man had lifted his wife's limp hands over her head and was struggling to push something down over those hands. Just like a mother puts a T-shirt or sweater on to a little child.

In the next few photographs, it seemed that the man was trying to dress up his wife's corpse for some bizarre reason—although the reason itself, and the outrageousness of it was slowly dawning upon both Maity and me, as we looked at each other between perusing the photos.

In the penultimate photograph, the man is seen at the window, curtains wide open, the light on the desk is on. But the ghastliest part of the image was the corpse of the woman on the bed, dressed in a grey raincoat, hair neatly done, face cleaned and looking calm and composed, eyes shut—almost as if she were asleep.

In the final and perhaps the most magnificent photograph among the ones we had seen so far in Sayantan Kundu's entire portfolio, the man is seen standing near the open door, his right arm wrapped around the waist of his dressed wife's corpse, her head softly resting on his shoulder and a hat covering her head and part of her face—the same hat we had seen in one of the earlier photographs. The man's left hand is extended towards the lamp on the writing desk and there's part of a couple of trolley suitcases visible just outside the doorway.

That was all. That was the last photograph. Maity and I let out our breaths together, completely exhausted, as Sayantan Kundu said in a grim voice: 'Didn't I tell you, Mr Maity? That's exactly what he did! He walked right past the reception in the lobby with the corpse of his wife!'

[5]

For a long period of time, there was pin-drop silence in the room. Maity was still shuffling through the photographs; I had sat down on the bed.

'How is that even possible?' I whispered. 'Wouldn't someone have seen him?'

'We will find out, soon enough,' muttered Maity, his eyes still on the photographs. 'Who is the other man?'

What! Was there another man in the photographs? Had I missed someone? I quickly went to Maity and tried to look at the photographs.

'What other man?' I asked.

'Not in these photographs,' said Maity, as he looked up at Sayantan. 'Two rooms across, to the left. Sitting at his desk right now, his right profile facing us? When did he check in?'

I realized Maity had seen someone through the camera. I hadn't. I went back to the camera, trying to see through it whom Maity was talking about.

'Oh, he's been there for a long time now,' said Sayantan. 'Three months at least.'

'Really?' I exclaimed, as I went back to the camera. 'Three months?'

'Writer?' I heard Maity's voice, as Sayantan adjusted the camera so I could take a look.

I knew that writers sometimes liked to work from the peace and solitude of a hotel room. Some of my own fellow writers whom I had met at literature festivals had told me that they just could not write from home. Fortunately, I've never had that problem.

'Yes, seems that way,' said Sayantan. 'He spends almost 90 per cent of his time on that desk, writing away. Writes by hand, doesn't type. Not sure what he's writing—perhaps a novel or something. Takes the occasional bathroom break, or lights up a cigarette once in a while, or reads a book. Wakes up late, works through the night. Leaves his room only twice a day—to have his meals at the café downstairs. Doesn't drink, doesn't have breakfast, doesn't shower or shave on most days. Once a week, the maid comes and cleans the room. He paces around in the corridor while she is in there. I have seen him scold the maid a couple of times, even asking her to leave. Quite rudely, as far as I could tell.'

I now saw the man in question. Young man, probably younger than Sayantan—in his mid-twenties or so. Slim build, thin hands. A head full of hair. Medium height. Dressed in shorts and a T-shirt that had become soaked in sweat just under the armpits. The man was seated at the edge of his chair and writing away on sheets of paper. A stack of sheets to his left—blank. Another stack to his right, a little away from him. Paper written on. Both stacks with paperweights on them. I saw him reach the end of the sheet he was writing on, keep it on the right stack, pull a blank page from the left bunch and continue writing. I noticed the pen in his hand—a fountain pen. The handwriting looked neat and beautiful, although a few words had been scratched out here and there, others underlined, yet others circled.

I looked around the room. A shirt dangling from a plastic hanger in the open wardrobe. A pair of slippers at the foot of the bed. A pair of shoes—Nike—on the floor near the wardrobe. A book on the nightstand, a small strip of tablets, a jug of water, a glass. Bed haphazardly made. One pillow used more than the other. I noticed a half-eaten apple peeping out of a dustbin in the corner of the room. The morning's newspaper had been slid under his door but not collected. The man put his pen down for a moment and stretched his back. Stared blankly at the wall in front of him for some time, then picked up the pen and started writing again.

'Okay,' said Maity. 'So he's been staying for a long time now. Which makes him interesting, because he might have information about the other guests. How about the other rooms? Any other regulars?'

'Well, not exactly like this man,' said Sayantan, 'but the room right next to his—the one between the writer's and the room where the murder happened—a middle-aged man comes there every month, for a week or so.'

'How long has he been coming now?'

'Three or four months, perhaps. Could be longer. I have seen him since I noticed the rooms. Always stays in the same room.'

'What does he do? Any idea?'

'He carries a suitcase around with him,' Sayantan showed us a few more photographs and pointed to a large beige-coloured old-fashioned Aristocrat suitcase. 'In it, he carries a few clothes; he seems quite particular about his clothes. Has them pressed by the hotel's bellboy who takes it to a washerman in a nearby lane and earns a neat tip. He also carries a few large books in his suitcase. Not sure what they are, but he carries them every single time he comes and stays.'

'Books?' Maity frowned.

'Yes,' said Sayantan. 'You'll find some of his photos in the bunch in your hands.'

'Do you have a magnifying glass in here somewhere?' Maity asked, as he looked at the relevant photos. The man seemed to be quite finicky and particular about his appearance. The entire room, too, bore signs of tidiness. Sayantan hurriedly picked up a magnifying glass from the shelf, and Maity peered into the photographs through the glass for a few seconds, at the end of which he muttered a single word, 'Encyclopaedias!'

'Salesman!' I exclaimed excitedly, and Maity gave me a soft pat of appreciation on my shoulder.

'Good job, Prakash! There's something else in that case of his, I can't get a clear look. Anyway, we will worry about that later. Let's not make any further delays. We are going to the Fairy Glen right now. And you, Mr Kundu, are coming with us!' Maity pointed towards Sayantan, who seemed quite hesitant and unwilling.

'Is it really necessary, Mr Maity?' he asked, with a look of appeal on his face. 'That I come with you?'

'Oh, it most certainly is!' said Maity, quite sternly. 'You will be a part of this investigation, this hunt, all throughout—from the beginning to the end. Even if the police need to get involved. You are a grown man, you knew the risks of the job before you took it, and you even knew the risks of coming to me with your disclosure and admission of guilt. You didn't think you would sit here in your room, all safe and cosy, while we run around the city tracking a murderer, did you? Get dressed, please. We will see you outside your door in two minutes. And if there are any more photographs that you think might be related to this case you have thrust upon me, then I suggest you bring them with you.'

Sayantan quickly picked up another yellow envelope and handed it over to Maity. Then he said, 'That's all I have. I didn't think these would be of much use to you, so . . .'

'Thank you,' said Maity and proceeded towards the door. 'See you outside.'

'Mr Maity,' said Sayantan, stopping Maity in his tracks. 'There's something else that we haven't discussed. Contrary to what you might think, I don't really earn too much from all this. I'm not quite sure if I will be able to afford your—'

Maity grimaced in irritation and said, 'Not everyone in the world thinks in terms of money, Mr Kundu. I most certainly do not. I know it's easy for me to say that because I come from a position of privilege, and you unfortunately don't. But let's just say, I am not a man for hire. Now let's not hold this up any longer, if you don't mind.'

Maity and I stepped into the corridor, and he immediately walked to the other end of it, near where the tube light was. I followed him. He quickly pulled out the other bunch of photographs that Sayantan Kundu had just handed over to him, and we looked down at the photos together, albeit in the flickering light.

What we were looking at now seemed to be a room on the top floor of the hotel—the same floor on which the honeymoon couple were staying. While the couple were staying to the extreme right, the north side of the hotel, there was another guest staying at the extreme left, the south side, towards Park Lane. The room he was staying in seemed to have a few things that the other rooms didn't: a television, a couch and even a small refrigerator. This man was bald, short and stout, wore red and black boxers, was shirtless and had layers and layers of fat on his body. His complexion was fair, his chubby hands always seemed to carry a television remote. In most of the photographs, he was seen sitting on the couch with his back to us, watching TV—mostly commercial Hindi movies. The only photographs of him where he was not on the couch in front of the TV were of him leaning in front of the fridge door holding a can of beer in his hand.

'Couch potato,' Maity mumbled. 'Seems like a slacker.'

'This is all becoming very confusing, Maity,' I said. 'Who stayed in which room, who checked in, who checked out, who does what, who's important, who's not? It's all jumbled up in my head.'

'You're right, Prakash,' said Maity. 'We'll need to draw up a nice little diagram of our snooping friend's point of view, so to speak. That'll make things simpler. It will also aid us in our investigation. He has thrust us into a dark and dirty world, and we can't see a thing around here. And imagine his gall! He thought he could sit it out!'

'Are you sure it's a good idea to take him along with us?' I asked. 'Don't you always say that everyone's a suspect? If we took him along, would he not go toe-to-toe with us, know what we are thinking?'

'We won't let him,' Maity said. 'From this point onwards, we need to be very careful about what we say or do in front of him. But if we keep him along with us, we will also know what *he* is thinking. Unless . . .'

'Unless?'

Sayantan Kundu had just stepped out into the corridor, and was looking here and there for us. When he saw us, he started walking towards us.

Maity stared at the young man's approaching figure for a second or two and said, 'Unless he is playing a game. A dangerous game that we just haven't fathomed. Come, Prakash! And remember, be on your guard. At all times!'

◻◻◻

Verdant, gently sloping hills, meandering brooks and streams flowing over polished pebbles strewn across sun-swept valleys, the Gaelic myths and lore of mystical night angels who descend from starry skies on clouds for wings, to bathe and frolic in those brooks deep in the woods—I presume such are the images that are likely to form in one's mind when one hears the words 'Fairy Glen'. *None* of the sights and sounds that stab you in the face when you enter the hotel of the same name in the heart of Kolkata correspond to those images. Like its neighbouring building, the hotel too may have seen some glory days in the time of the Raj. The name itself was distinctively Scottish. But other than one or two rare remnant signs of magnificence peeping at you from here and there, nothing about the hotel seemed to have anything to do with either fairies or green glens.

The hotel itself was comprised of four floors. The ground floor had the lobby with a small sitting area—two sofas and a table placed next to an old fireplace—and the reception, where in this digital day and age, a frail-looking sexagenarian Anglo-Indian man was standing between a huge guest register and a wall with keys dangling from hooks against room numbers and peering over the thick lenses of his ancient-looking spectacles at a magazine photograph of Rod Stewart. As we later found out, the rest of the ground floor housed the kitchen and the restaurant, both of which were like the fireplace in the lobby. In other words, defunct. The guest rooms were all on the first, second and third floors of the building, above which was the terrace, the door to which was permanently kept under lock and key. The hotel had fifteen 'Executive' rooms and three 'Suite' rooms. The difference between the two categories was the inclusion of a colour television, a couch and a refrigerator. Maity and I had seen one of the suite rooms in the photographs—this was the one in which the couch potato was staying. The receptionist gentleman, whose name was Malcolm Brennan, further told us that the hotel also boasted of a special 'Honeymoon Suite', with certain added privileges. We learnt all this info not at once, but bit by bit, over the next couple of hours, as Maity wove yet another of his magic spells. In fact, in the beginning, when the receptionist learnt that we had no interest in taking a room, and that we were only looking for some information, he was reluctant to even speak to us. Maity had expected this, and had come prepared.

'Look, Mr Brennan,' he said to the frowning old man, 'I'm not looking for any trouble. Nor am I here to cause any. Certainly not the kind that was so unnecessarily and undeservingly brought upon you and the other members of the staff here during that scandal last year. Yes, that one! With the minister and his . . . companions. How old were those girls again? You would imagine that elected representatives of the people would know better! But no! What can ordinary men like you and I do or say, tell me?'

'Who are you again?' the old man's frown grew deeper.

'My name is Janardan Maity. You may know Father Lobo, who leads the parish in the Seventh Day Adventist nearby? He's a good friend of mine.'

'Father Drew?' responded Mr Brennan, 'Andrew Lobo?'

'Good man,' Maity nodded. 'You can ask him about me. He'll vouch for me.'

'Father Lobo told you about the . . . incident with the politician fellow?'

'Oh, no, no, no!' Maity clarified with a smile that told me he was lying through his teeth. 'He is a man doing the Lord's good work. He cannot be bothered with such things! No, I know all this because, let's just say, it is my job to know such things. Also, in my nature!'

'Are you a cop or something?'

'No sir, I'm not with the police,' Maity deliberately hesitated and smiled genially. 'But not entirely unrelated either. You could say the police have had some help from me, and I from them, from time to time. It is a—how shall I say—a relationship that thrives on symbiosis, if you see what I mean? That, and mutual respect!'

'What do you want?' Mr Brennan grunted.

'I just want some information about some of your guests,' said Maity. 'And perhaps a quick visit to a couple of the rooms. Not the ones that are occupied—I don't want to disturb your guests. Just the ones that are vacant, and just a couple of them. Shouldn't be any trouble at all for you.'

'You got a search warrant on you, son?'

The smile on Maity's face slowly disappeared, and what remained was only a chilling stare directly into the old man's eyes. I had seen that deadly stare make even the

most dangerous criminals shudder in their shoes. Malcolm
Brennan was just a poor old ordinary man trying to make a
living manning a dingy old hotel in the heart of the city.

'No, Mr Brennan.' Like his facial expression, Maity's
voice too had changed, 'As a matter of fact, I do not. But
I could very well go get one and come back. Trouble is, if
and when I do, I would not be able to come back by myself.
I would not be alone, is all I am saying. The matter would be
out of my hands—if you catch my drift? And I am a benevolent
man, by nature. I do not want that to happen. Nor do my
friends and trusted companions here. It is not in our agenda
that any harm should come upon a respectable man such as
you, doing his best to run a respectable business such as this
splendid hotel.'

'We try to keep it clean,' the man somehow managed to
put in a few words in the face of Maity's verbal volley.

'Of course, you do! Hell, I can put a handsome wager on
that claim of yours! But mankind, Mr Brennan!' Maity raised
his arms and made a scary face. 'Greed and lust ruling this
world like there is just no shore in sight. Take that oaf of a
minister, for instance. Or all those people who come in here
and do dealings that cannot be called legal in the strictest
sense of the term now, do they? Do you think they know?
Or bother?'

Maity lowered his voice and stooped towards the man,
'Why just the other day, a man came in here with a case full
of that vile white powder. Would you believe that?'

'How am I . . .'

'How on *earth* are you supposed to know that,
Mr Brennan?' Maity's voice rose several decibels and startled
the old man. 'How in the name of the good lord, I ask

you? Mankind! A roost is all they need for their vile acts of greed. And lust! Let's not forget that. Did you know that the honeymoon couple who came in here three months ago, they had a camera with them?'

'That's their business!'

'Of course, it is!' Maity suddenly lowered his voice and drew closer to the aged receptionist. 'But bad for *your* business too, isn't it, sir?'

The man showed the first signs of breaking. 'What do you want?' And Maity pounced in.

'Just a tour of your second and third floors, and a glance at that majestic-looking register of yours. Perhaps the answers to a few additional questions, and I will be out of your . . . hair.'

Malcolm Brennan sighed, turned the register around, pushed it towards Maity and walked away without saying a single word.

'You were brilliant, Mr Maity!' whispered Sayantan Kundu with a big smile, and was shocked by the reaction of the man he had just addressed. As was I. Maity pushed him away and said in a low, whispering voice, 'You shut the hell up! What should have been done in a legal, formal, decent way is being done in secrecy, as if *I* am the thief here. All because I have to protect *you*! You think I enjoy making a fool out of that old man? Or to threaten him like that?'

Sayantan Kundu was at a complete loss for words. Maity was still fuming. I quickly stepped forward and opened the register, flipping the pages carefully.

'What dates are we looking at, Maity?' I asked.

Maity turned to me and calmed down a bit, as there was work to be done and no time to be wasted.

'Start with at least five days before the night of the murder,' he said.

'Till?'

'Today.'

As my cell phone's camera continued to flash and Maity continued to turn the pages of the register, I couldn't help but ask him, 'How did you know about all these scandals at this hotel?'

'You remember Satish? He is posted at Park Street Police Station these days,' said Maity. 'Before you woke up, I paid him a visit during my morning walk. His quarters are in New Alipore, not too far from my home.'

I knew Maity had several contacts in the police department. Senior Inspector Satish Mukherjee was one of them. Maity and he had worked on a complex murder case in Jadavpur once, and had been friends ever since. This was well before I had met Maity. But I had met Inspector Satish and his wife once when they had come to visit me at Maity's home. His wife had read some of my novels, and I had signed a few books for her.

'You told him what we are doing?' I asked.

'Not exactly,' Maity said, as he turned the last page, marked with today's date. 'He knows me, he will never ask. But he knows about this visit. We can't afford to keep the police entirely in the dark. After all, a murder has been committed! And no matter what this photographer fellow says or thinks, at some stage, we will have to involve Satish.'

Malcolm Brennan walked out of a room, the door of which carried the word 'Gentlemen' on it. He came over to the reception counter. Maity gently turned the register around and pushed it towards him.

'Thank you, Mr Brennan!'

'Anything else you'd like to bother me with?'

'Yes!' grinned Maity, looking painfully shameless. 'Just a quick tour of a few rooms!'

[6]

The next morning, I woke up later than usual, but took a quick shower and waited for Maity to come, as he had promised to meet me at around eleven. I had gone home to my Ballygunge residence after our visit to the Fairy Glen. Maity had sent Sayantan Kundu home and said that he would call him soon. After that, Maity had dropped me home and asked me to spend the rest of the day gleaning all the information from the register, collect it in one neat bunch and share it with him. When I had asked him where he was headed, he said that he wanted to go home and take a closer look at all the photographs again. I did as he had told me and was exhausted by the evening. To be honest, so much half-baked information had been thrown at us in such a short period of time that everything was a foggy blur to me. But I also knew that Maity was a man of his word and that he had promised to make everything clear soon. So I made a conscious decision not to think about the entire thing any more, had an early dinner and went to bed. I had a feeling that as soon as my head hit the pillow, I must have fallen asleep.

Maity came exactly at eleven. It was good to see him smiling again. He plonked down on one of the chairs in my drawing room and remained silent for a while, the smile still playing on his lips. I sat opposite him, waiting for him to speak.

'A photograph is a secret about a secret,' he said. 'The more it tells you, the less you know!'

I was wondering how to respond to that, when he asked: 'Do you know who said that?'

I didn't. Maity smiled and said, 'Diane Arbus. American photographer. Remarkable woman! Remarkable life! Albeit with a sad ending.'

'Does that mean you learnt more from the photographs last night?' I asked. 'Or less?'

Maity said, 'Conventional wisdom, such as the one seemingly possessed by the current generation to which you belong, would think of answers as knowledge. But speak to the greatest philosophers and scientists the world has known, and they will all tell you otherwise. They will say that the birth of a new question in your mind is perhaps more important than finding the right answers. Answers . . . they will come, one way or the other, sooner or later. If we keep looking, inevitably they will come. It is the questions that don't come so often. And therein lies the problem.'

I smiled and looked at my dear old friend. He seemed happy this morning. And somewhat content with himself. This is how I liked seeing him—not in a foul mood, grumbling and complaining.

'Your smile is doing little to hide your impatience, my friend,' said Maity. 'So, let's try and make things a little clearer for you.'

Having said this, Maity proceeded to pull a sheet of paper from his bag and handed it over to me, 'There you go!' I looked at the sheet. On it was a sketch, sort of a diagram, of the view of the six rooms of the Fairy Glen that were visible from Sayantan Kundu's peephole. Against each room, Maity had made some notes. The diagram looked something like this:

301 Harish Jhunjhunwala Check-in: 9 Jun Check-out: 21 Jun	302 Vacant	303 Kishore & Riya Rajbanshi Check-in: 19 Jun Check-out: 20 Jun
201 T. Subramaniam Check-in:??? Check-out: Staying	202 Jayant Sinha Check-in: 16 Jun Check-out: Staying	203 Robert & Edith Sullivan Check-in: 18 Jun Check-out: 20 Jun

Snapshot of guests staying at Hotel Fairy Glen on the night of 19 Jun. Diagram made on 27 Jun.

I studied the diagram for a long time, and Maity waited patiently. When I finally looked up at him, I found him staring at me.

'Well?' he asked.

'Impressive!' I responded. 'It's much clearer now. Although, I have to agree with you that this now raises more questions than answers.'

'For instance?' asked Maity, with interest.

'For instance, the most obvious question staring us right in the face is, when did Mr Subramaniam check into the Fairy Glen?'

Maity smiled for a few seconds. And then he said, 'Is that really the first thing you noticed?'

I looked at the diagram again. 'Why, is there something else?'

'Of course!' Maity rose from his chair and said: 'Why did the honeymoon couple leave the very next morning? When they clearly had a reservation for three nights, as confirmed by the receptionist? Did they hear or see anything suspicious? On the night of the murder? Remember they were trying to listen to what was going on in the room below? Don't forget, we are only looking at photographs— still images, frozen in time. We know nothing about what any of them were doing or experiencing at any point of time outside those photographs.'

I thought about it for a second. Maity had a point.

'There's more!' he said. 'Mr Jhunjhunwala sits around watching movies all day, doesn't go out, even for a second, has his meals delivered to his room, cleans his room himself, doesn't allow anyone to enter his room. We learnt all that from the receptionist yesterday, didn't we? And this peculiar behaviour of the man continued for as many as twelve days. Why? What is Harish Jhunjhunwala's profession? What does he do? *Who is he?*'

'What do you think he does?'

'I haven't the faintest idea! But I can think of at least one reason that explains his behaviour.'

'He is hiding!' I exclaimed.

'Exactly!' Maity said. 'He doesn't want to be seen. He has— as they say in the movies—gone underground. And then, just like that, he checks out one fine day and disappears! *Why?*'

I frowned and thought about the entire affair. Maity was right. The problem wasn't as easy as I had imagined it to be. Maity was far from done though.

'T. Subramaniam,' he said. 'You are wondering *when* he checked in. That question is irrelevant—we know Sayantan had seen him from the first day itself. We know he is a writer, the receptionist confirmed that. He said the young man was writing a novel. But don't you see the more mysterious affair going on in his room?'

I was at a complete loss for words. 'What mysterious affair?' I asked blankly.

Maity seemed quite taken aback. He said, 'Didn't you see him through the camera, writing?'

'I—yes . . . yes, I did . . .'

'And yet, you didn't see?' Maity looked shocked. 'You are a writer yourself, Prakash. How could you have missed this?'

I just didn't know what to say. So I figured it would be best to remain silent and let Maity explain.

'The handwriting!' Maity said. 'His letters are microscopic, to say the least. It was only on the highest level of zoom that I could read what he was writing. And although his handwriting is tiny in size, he was writing away quite furiously, at a surprisingly fast pace.'

'That can happen, what is the problem with that?' I contested. 'Why, it happens to me quite often. Not as often as I would like it to, though! But I think that's a good thing to happen to a writer. Any writer!'

'No, no, no, no, no!' Maity shook his head vehemently and almost yelled out, 'You are missing my point altogether. If Mr Subramaniam is writing so fast in such a small font size, that too for over three months, then imagine what his *output* must be. Imagine the length of his novel.'

I was still hesitating. I could see the reason behind Maity's doubt, but for some reason, I was sure there was a reasonable explanation to the entire thing.

'Perhaps he is writing a voluminous piece of work? Perhaps a really lengthy novel. I mean, that's not impossible, is it?'

'It's not, certainly not. Unless he is writing—by my calculations—a novel with 10,000 pages!'

'But,' I argued, 'I'm sure it's not always that he is blessed with that kind of pace. Perhaps he has phases of writer's block too, who knows?'

'Well, in that case, Sayantan would have told us as much, don't you think? Don't forget what he said—that young man spends 90 per cent of his waking time *writing* away. Not thinking, not waiting for a plot, not planning, but writing. And that makes me wonder. What exactly is he writing?'

I thought for a few seconds and made up my mind. This had to be addressed.

'Can I tell you something, Maity?' I said. 'You may be good at deduction, but as you yourself said, I am a writer myself. You are good at your job, but I am not so bad at mine either. I can assure you that you are reading too much into it.'

Maity looked like he had suddenly hit a wall while walking down a street. He stared at me for some time and a soft smile appeared on his face. Then he said, 'Very well, let's move on!'

'I hope you didn't mind my saying that?' I asked.

'Oh, no, no, my friend! You are right. Getting stuck on a single piece is not a good habit in puzzle-solving. Sometimes, rotating the picture and looking at it from a different perspective helps, gives us a new direction to think in, a whole new clue. But there is one last oddity that I noticed in the diagram, and I have to share it with you—because it seems you haven't noticed it thus far. It will give you something to think about. And perhaps you can tell me if this is also something that I am overthinking. A figment of my imagination!'

'What is that?'

'Do you remember what Sayantan had told us about the encyclopaedia salesman, Mr Jayant Sinha?'

'More or less, yes,' I tried to summon every bit of information I had heard from Sayantan Kundu about the gentleman.

'Specifically, what did he tell us about the frequency of his visits to the Fairy Glen?'

'Oh yes!' I exclaimed, 'How could I have missed that? He comes on the same day every month and stays exactly for a week!'

'And yet, he is *still* there!' said Maity. 'Most salespeople have a fixed, regimented schedule. But it's almost been a week since Mr Sinha ought to have left.'

'But he hasn't.'

'But he hasn't. This time, he hasn't. *Why?*'

I nodded. Maity certainly had a point. But I now had something to add of my own, by way of contributing to this investigation.

'Maity, there's something I must tell you about the one room that we haven't spoken about at all,' I said.

'You mean the vacant room?'

'Yes,' I said. 'As I was collecting the information from the register last night so that I could share the summary with you, I missed telling you that although that particular room was vacant on the night of the murder, there was a check-in that morning.'

A frown appeared on Maity's forehead and stayed there. 'What check-in?'

'Hang on a second,' I consulted my notes. 'Someone named Mrs Daisy Zorabian.'

'Why didn't you tell me this before?' Maity was clearly unhappy. 'When did she check in?'

'On the morning of the nineteenth. Around half past eleven.'

'The day of the murder!' Maity exclaimed. 'And checked out?'

'She checked out that very evening, at 4 p.m.'

Maity was lost in his thoughts. I heard him whisper a single word: 'Strange!'

'Probably she just needed to rest for a few hours?' I suggested a possibility.

Maity looked at me and said, 'You mean, for instance, if she had come to Kolkata by flight and had a train to catch later that evening? Or vice versa? Something of that sort?'

'Yes,' I said. 'That could be one explanation. Or who knows, perhaps someone from her family or a friend came to know that she was in town, came over to the hotel and whisked her away to their home. There could be many possible explanations, Maity.'

'Right! But only one of them really happened!' Maity said, still lost in thought. I realized that I shouldn't have missed out on giving him this seemingly vital piece of information, but it also seemed to me that his quest for a reasonable explanation to Mrs Zorabian's strange behaviour had made him forget my mistake, at least temporarily. I quickly seized this opportunity of his absent-mindedness and said, 'Shall I update the diagram with this information?'

'No,' he shook his head. 'It's a snapshot, remember? Of the night of the murder. Of only those guests who were staying in those specific rooms at the exact time when the murder took place. Unless, of course . . .'

Maity pinched his lips and frowned hard.

'Unless?'

'Nah,' he came out of his trance. 'Just a vague thought, nothing important. Let's go. We've already lost a lot of time!'

'Where are we going?' I asked.

Maity picked up his bag from the table, put the sling on his shoulder and said, 'To catch a killer!'

□□□

Salkia was a residential part of Howrah. But like most neighbourhoods of Howrah, it was congested and buzzing with activity. When our cab was crossing over the Hooghly via the Howrah Bridge, I asked Maity why on earth would he expect Robert Sullivan to still be at his residence after having committed his wife's murder and disposing of her corpse. Instead of answering my question, Maity had asked me to go through my notes and confirm the man's address again.

'53-D, Kerestanpara, Salkia,' I said.

Sayantan Kundu was sitting in the front seat, next to the driver. We had picked him up from his home. This was also an opportunity for Maity and me to take another look at the six rooms of the Fairy Glen through Sayantan's camera. All three rooms of the top floor were still vacant, as was the room on the second floor in which the crime had taken place. Jayant Sinha's room was dark too, but we could see some of his stuff still neatly arranged in his room. Which meant that he hadn't checked out yet. Finally, in Room 201, Mr Subramaniam, the writer, was sitting at his desk, hunched over his sheets and writing away.

'The name Kerestanpara must have come because a lot of Christians lived in the neighbourhood, isn't it?'

Maity nodded at Sayantan's question and shut his eyes to enjoy the cool breeze over the river. I remembered he had said that he hadn't got any sleep the night before last. I hoped he got some last night and wasn't staring at those photographs till the crack of dawn.

'This gentleman,' Maity said, his eyes still shut, 'Jayant Sinha. Have you ever seen anyone come to his room?'

I realized the question was addressed to Sayantan, who thought for a few seconds and said, 'Other than the bellboy, no one. The boy does a few odd jobs for him. You know, gets a bottle of soda from around the corner, takes his clothes for pressing to the next lane, brings him his meals.'

'He has his meals in his room?'

'Every single night,' said Sayantan. 'The man seems extremely disciplined. Wakes up early in the morning to an alarm. Goes to bed early.'

'An alarm?' I interrupted. 'You mean like a physical alarm clock?'

'No, must be an alarm on his cell phone.'

I said, 'Then how do you know he wakes up to an alarm? I thought you said you couldn't hear anything from those rooms?'

'Let me guess,' said Maity, his eyes still shut. 'He woke up at exactly the same time every morning?'

'Sharp at seven,' said Sayantan. 'Is very particular about his dinner time too. Sharp at 8 p.m.'

'What time does he go to bed?'

'After dinner, he sits with some of his notebooks and documents—seems like he is keeping accounts of some sort. Sometimes he writes something in his diary or reads something and then makes a call or two. At exactly ten at night, he wraps up everything, switches off the lights and goes to bed.'

'When does he drink?'

'Excuse me?' Sayantan turned around to look at Maity. His face seemed confused.

Maity opened his eyes and said, 'You said he sometimes asks the bellboy to get soda bottles for him, from the shops downstairs or around the corner. That would mean he drinks?'

'Oh yes,' Sayantan seemed to remember. 'Sometimes, not every night!'

Having said this much, Sayantan turned back around to face the street. Maity stared at the back of Sayantan's head for some time and then slowly said, 'Is he able to sell anything? Get any orders?'

'That I can't say,' responded the young man. 'To be honest, it was only when you said that those books were encyclopaedias that I came to know he was a salesman. I thought he must have brought them with him to read.'

I looked at Maity to gauge his reaction to what Sayantan had just said. But I found him looking out of the window.

'In all these days,' said Maity, in a gentle, faraway voice, 'have you ever seen him read?'

Sayantan seemed to be at a loss for words. With a smile of embarrassment, he said, 'You're right, I haven't.'

Kerestanpara was a dingy road running perpendicular to the river, far from the lines of factories and warehouses along the western shore of the Hooghly. Half the shops on the road were those that sold or repaired musical instruments. Guitars, accordions, violins, drums, congas, clarinets—Maity even pointed out a piano tuner in one corner. Mostly Western-style musical instruments. Very rarely, I could see a sitar here or a tabla there. Also lining both sides of the road were grocers, bakeries, tailoring shops, decidedly unreliable-looking pharmacies and even seedy shoe stores. Shops downstairs, residences upstairs. We found 53-D to be a small apartment on the second floor above a store that sold all kinds of chinaware. But when we reached the apartment itself, there was a lock hanging on the front door.

'They've gone home,' informed the middle-aged lady living in the next apartment, 53-C, on seeing us standing in front of her neighbour's door.

'The Sullivans?' Maity asked. 'Aren't they from around here?'

'Bob and Edith,' said the lady, still running a comb down her long strands of hair that almost reached the frilly edge of her skirt. 'They are from Bangalore. Said they will spend the summer there. Said summers are pleasant there. Here, half the time the power is out. Stay a few minutes, you'll see for yourself.'

'When did they leave?' Maity asked.

'It's been one or two weeks,' she replied.

'One week or two weeks?' Sayantan asked.

With a gesture of his hand, Maity asked him to leave the questioning to himself and took a couple of steps towards the lady. 'We are friends of Robert. Can you remember exactly when he left for Bangalore?'

'Let's see.' The woman looked up at the ceiling and continued combing. 'I had my weekly off at the hospital the next day. So, must be Monday. Yes, I remember now, it was Monday.'

'Last Monday?'

'No, no! The Monday before that.'

'The eighteenth of June?'

'Is that what it was?' she said, 'Yes, Monday eighteenth.'

Maity and I exchanged glances. Maity then turned to the lady and asked, 'And Edith was with him when he left?'

'What do you mean?' pat came the reply. 'Why will he leave without his wife? You don't quarrel with your wife or what? Do you leave her and go away? Bob doesn't speak too much. But he is not that kind of guy. They don't have a child, no? Nor do they have the money for all those treatments. So Edith is sometimes in a bad mood. Bob yells too, but only once in a while. Edith yells more. I tell her, it's not okay the way you treat that man. One day, he will lose it. Men who are quiet are like . . . like volcanoes, you know? Calm outside. Boiling inside. Not fair, I tell her. I don't care, I tell the truth. She can be my friend, or she can be the President of the country. I don't spare anyone. No matter who it is, I will—'

'Has Robert come back to the apartment after that day?' Maity interrupted the lady gently. 'Perhaps he forgot something? Or for any other reason?'

'Why will he come back?'

'Perhaps the next day itself, or the morning of the twentieth? Two days after he had left.'

The woman shook her head and simply said, 'No!'

Maity looked at the lock on the door and then looked at me. I knew how much he wanted to break that door open and take a look inside. But there was no way to do that. Certainly not under the circumstances. He shut his eyes for a second to regain his composure, then turned around to thank the lady and walked past me and Sayantan towards the staircase.

'Too late!' I heard him mutter under his breath, as I followed him. 'The bird has flown the coop!'

We made our way downstairs and boarded the cab. I looked up to find the lady staring down at us from the balcony with a frown on her forehead.

'What now, Maity?' I asked, as our cab rolled out of the dingy road and reached a less congested part of the neighbourhood.

'Park Lane,' Maity told the driver. 'Take the Vidyasagar Setu this time.'

'I . . . I can take a bus . . .' mumbled Sayantan Kundu. 'You don't have to drop me.'

'I'm not dropping you,' growled Maity. 'Not for a while.'

'Then where are we going, Maity?' I asked.

As our cab reached Grand Trunk Road and picked up speed, Maity's grave voice was heard over the sound of traffic, 'Café Columbus!'

[7]

In less than an hour, we found ourselves standing in front of Café Columbus on Park Lane. It was directly across the street from the Fairy Glen. The place seemed to get really busy during lunch hours, but Maity had anticipated that and made a reservation from the cab itself. A waiter took us to a table for three in the corner of the café, diagonally opposite to the entrance. Maity looked around and said, 'Perfect!'

I looked at the menu and said, 'Oh, they have crepes!'

'What?' Maity had perhaps not heard me, because the din inside the café was quite loud. I raised my voice and repeated what I had said.

'We are not here to eat!'

Those few words, and the way Maity said them, sent my heart thumping. Because as I looked up at him, I saw that his eyes were fixed on something. Or someone. I turned around to follow his gaze.

Although his back was towards us, the hunched stature, the head full of hair, the reed-thin hands and the wet armpits of his light-yellow shirt were unmistakable. Our writer friend, Mr T. Subramaniam, was having his lunch in one corner of the café, facing the glass wall. Just outside the wall was the busy footpath, where a constant stream of people was rushing past in both directions. Mr Subramaniam's eyes, however, were focused on a book he was reading while munching on his food.

'Surely you're not thinking of going and speaking to him, are you?' Sayantan Kundu asked Maity that question in a voice that reminded me of a sacrificial lamb. He cast a pleading glance at Maity, only to be rudely held by his arm and dragged towards the other corner of the café by none other than Maity himself. I picked up my phone from the table and hurriedly followed them.

'Mr Subramaniam?' Maity said, in as polite a voice as he could summon under the clamorous circumstances, 'My name is Janardan Maity. This is my friend Prakash Ray, he is an author, you may have heard about him or read his books. And this is Sayantan Kundu, who lives right down the lane. May we join you?'

Mr Subramaniam looked at us by turns and then stared at me.

'I don't believe this!' he said with a mixture of surprise and suspicion in his eyes. 'You are Prakash Ray? Of course I've read your books. Not all of them though. I'm sorry, but what is this about?'

Maity slid into the sofa opposite Mr Subramaniam and asked, 'Oh, that's lovely! Which one have you *not* read?'

By this time, I had also quickly taken a seat beside Maity. Sayantan Kundu was still looking around, and on finding an unoccupied chair at a table nearby, claimed it, dragged it up and settled down, looking extremely uncomfortable with this clearly unexpected meeting.

'Excuse me!' Maity summoned a waiter passing by. 'Three coffees please, strong!'

'What is all this about?' the young writer asked again.

'Mr Subramaniam,' Maity edged forward in his seat and placed his two elbows on the table in a prohibitively counter-etiquette manner, 'you strike me as an exceptionally intelligent man. Just like my friend Prakash here. All writers are inherently intelligent people, they are keen observers and thinkers. They like to soak things in, like a sponge. Exactly the kind of people that are to my liking. Which is why, I'm not going to beat around the bush with you. With others, I might have—but not with you. With you, I want to come straight to the point, if you will permit me to do so.'

Mr Subramaniam glanced at our faces again with a suspicious and cautious look, kept his fork down on his plate, placed a bookmark on the page he was reading, closed the book and said, 'I'm sorry, who are you again?'

'Eight days ago,' Maity went on, 'on the night of Tuesday, the nineteenth of June, there was a murder in one of the rooms of Hotel Fairy Glen. Yes, the same one you are staying in. Now, unlike most murders, this particular one hasn't been discovered yet. Except by Mr Kundu here, who witnessed the murder through his window right across the lane.'

I had expected a look of alarm and withdrawal to appear on Mr Subramaniam's face. Instead, he looked at Sayantan Kundu and simply said, 'Is it possible that you might be . . . I don't know . . . mistaken?'

'May I ask why you say so?' Maity said.

'Well,' Mr Subramaniam shuffled in his seat, 'had there been a murder in the hotel I am staying in, that too more than a week ago, wouldn't the hotel folks have informed me about it? I mean, it's not just a question of the news of the incident. It's a question about the safety of the guests too, isn't it? I don't understand what you are telling me.'

'You are absolutely correct!' Maity responded. 'It's a little difficult to understand. But like I told you, this murder has not been discovered yet, by anyone. Except by Mr Kundu here. And then, he told me about it.'

Mr Subramaniam stared at Sayantan Kundu for a long time with an expression of incredulity floating on his face. Then he asked, 'And you *saw* this murder happen?'

'Yes!' I could sense that Sayantan was trying his best to keep his voice steady.

'With your own eyes?'

'It was quite by accident that he had to witness this . . . this . . . scene,' Maity came to Sayantan Kundu's rescue. 'It was quite late in the night, and Mr Kundu had risen from his bed to go to the bathroom, when he saw this.'

'And who was murdered, you said?'

'A lady,' said Maity, 'by the name of Edith Sullivan.'

The tension around the table was unreal, to say the least. From the corner of my eye, I could see Sayantan trying to keep his hands steady. The young writer was still taking turns to look at our faces one by one, trying to gauge what exactly we wanted from him, or—worse still—if we were trying to pull some sort of prank on him.

'Okay,' he finally said. 'I sort of keep to myself though, so I can't see how I could . . . you know . . . help you?'

'We are aware of that,' Maity said calmly, 'but . . .'

'Hang on, you are aware of that?' Mr Subramaniam's voice changed suddenly. 'What do you mean? Have you been asking around about me? Am I a suspect, somehow?'

'No, no, Mr Subramaniam,' Maity tried to calm him down. 'Let me assure you . . .'

'I keep to myself! I'm in my room, all the time! Okay? Please understand that. I don't even know who's been . . .

murdered . . . this lady . . . or whoever . . . why are you even talking to me about all this?'

'To seek your help,' replied Maity. 'That's all!'

'Help? What kind of help?'

'For whatever it's worth, you are in a unique position to help us, Mr Subramaniam. You have been staying in that hotel for over three months now. We have seen the register, spoken to the receptionist. We understand you've been writing a novel. But unfortunately, this murder has happened on your floor, just a couple of rooms across yours.'

Mr Subramaniam placed his thin, bloodless fingers on his lips, without saying a word. That he was feeling decidedly uncomfortable about all this was quite evident, but it was also true that he kept his calm. He came across to me as a strong individual on the inside, despite his outward appearance. There was a look of maturity in his expressions, and I knew very well that Maity would not attempt, nor succeed in trying, to break him the way he had threatened the receptionist at the hotel. No, this was a man who had to be dealt with differently, carefully. And I was waiting with bated breath to see how Maity would approach the situation. The coffees had come, and I picked mine up and took a sip. Sayantan Kundu looked like he had no strength left in him, and that unless someone picked up his cup and literally made him take a sip, the beverage would remain in its vessel and be wasted.

'Are you with the police?' Mr Subramaniam finally asked.

'Well,' Maity hesitated, 'not exactly . . .'

'Mr Janardan Maity is a renowned private detective,' I stepped in. 'He is trying to solve the case of this murder and apprehend the killer.'

'A detective?' Mr Subramaniam asked. 'You mean like a private investigator? Like . . . like Sherlock Holmes?'

Maity raised his hand uncomfortably and said, 'May I just say that those points are irrelevant here, Mr Subramaniam? What is important is that we ask you if you have heard or seen anything suspicious in the hotel over the last couple of weeks or so.'

'Suspicious?' Mr Subramaniam scoffed. 'It's a hotel! A cheap one at that. Everything is suspicious. Walls are thin, so are floors and ceilings. You sneeze in one room, you get heard in the next. Babies crying in the middle of the night, people screaming at each other, loud parties, drunken brawls, men grunting, women moaning, I could go on and on. It's a dump!'

'And yet you are staying there?'

'Yeah! I am writing a novel!'

'Doesn't the noise bother you?'

'Nope! I could sit in this café and write. Or out there, in the middle of the street. I have, in fact. In this café, I mean. Not on the street! You see, I can't say whether I am a good writer or not—that is for the readers to judge. But I do have another gift. And that is, once I start writing, nothing bothers me. I can't hear a thing. I'm in my own world. You could burst a firecracker or conduct a symphony right next to my ears, and I wouldn't notice.'

'I envy you,' I said casually.

'Oh no!' Mr Subramaniam turned to me. 'I envy *you*! Yes sir, I do! You are really good! I've read quite a few of your books, and I must say I admire your writing. Perhaps you could give me a few tips? Not on writing though. That I am told I have a flair for. On getting my novel published, when it's complete. That's a tough one to crack, that game. But how come you are, you know, here? You aren't with the police too, are you? Or . . . oh! Wait a minute! Are you friends with this gentleman?'

'I am.'

'Oh!' A smile crept on to the young man's face. 'Like an assistant, like Watson . . . or . . . or Hastings! Wow! I've never . . . you know . . . met a real-life detective and his assistant before!'

Maity couldn't take the mention of that word any more. I, of all people, knew how much he hated being called a detective. He quickly interjected, 'Prakash is a dear friend. You say you are not bothered by the noise and the ruckus at all?'

'No, sir, never have.'

'Then why do you write in a hotel room, Mr Subramaniam?'

'Ah! A very detective-like question!' The man smiled. Maity shut his eyes in agony.

'Well, because I like the solitude. Also, because I wrote my previous novel in that hotel, in the same room. I couldn't get that one published, though. Sent it to a bunch of publishers, most of them never bothered to respond. Some responded with a standard rejection template. I know the room, and I like it. I mean, I don't *enjoy* living there, but then I cannot imagine a place in the world where I *would* enjoy living!'

'When did you check in?'

'This time? Let's see, sometime in March, I think. Late March. Yeah! The last time was more than a year ago, when I was writing my previous novel.'

'And you don't know this lady?' Maity extended a photograph of Edith Sullivan towards Mr Subramaniam.

I heard the chair beside me creak and looked up at Sayantan Kundu to find that he was sweating profusely. With a gesture of my eyes, I asked him to calm down. In my mind, I knew that there was no reason for him to be nervous because the photograph was a close-up. There was no way to know that it had been taken in one of the rooms of the Fairy Glen.

'I've seen her,' came the response from Subramaniam. 'I was going down the stairs, she was coming up; there was another man with her—presumably her husband. Big, tall man. I had to stand aside to let the bellboy pass with the luggage. They had a couple of suitcases with them, as far as I can remember.'

'Did you talk?'

'Did I talk? To her? No! I just greeted them. Not even greeted—one of those courteous nods of the head, you know?'

'And that's the last you saw of either of them?'

'The first and the last. My omelette is getting cold. Would you mind if I ate as we spoke?'

Maity and I quickly exchanged glances. Why did the man suddenly seem at such ease? Was he not bothered at all by the fact that something as serious as a murder had happened two doors across his room?

'Not at all,' said Maity. 'Was this the man who was staying with her?'

The young man looked at the photograph that Maity had showed him and said, 'Yes, that's the gentleman. Not sure if he was staying with her, though. But he was the one who was coming up the stairs with her.'

'What can you tell us about some of the other guests in the hotel?'

'Well, like I said, I keep to myself mostly. There's a couple on the first floor, who are always yelling and swearing at each other, that too in the filthiest words possible. Room's just beside the stairs, so one can hear them while coming up or going down. I think they live in an apartment somewhere close by. I had heard one of the other guests complaining to the receptionist about them. The poor old receptionist has to field such complaints all day long, you know? Good old man, name's Malcolm. I heard him tell the complaining guest that the couple causing the nuisance were there because of some construction going on in their apartment, and that they would be gone soon. And they were!'

'When did this happen?'

'Around a month or so ago.'

'I see,' said Maity. 'Anyone else?'

Mr Subramaniam thought for a few seconds and said: 'There's a violinist who seems to be staying in one of the rooms. I think on the top floor. Or could be on the floor below mine, I'm not quite sure. He or she's been here for a couple of weeks. I've never really seen him or her. I have only heard the violin played. And there's a salesman of some kind, who comes and stays in the room next to mine every once in a while. He seems to be a regular.'

'This man?' Maity showed him a photograph of Jayant Sinha.

'That's the man, yes.'

'Have you met him?'

'Seen him in the hall,' said Mr Subramaniam. 'Never spoken to him. Except maybe this one time when he had asked me for matches.'

'No complaints either?'

'Excuse me?' Mr Subramaniam had perhaps not understood the question.

'No noise or botheration from his room?' Maity clarified. 'You are right next door!'

'Oh, no, no, no! When he stays in that room, I don't hear any noise. Probably because he's out most of the day anyway.'

'How do you know that he's out most of the day?'

I looked at Maity to find a very familiar steely look on his face. The response from Mr. Subramaniam came a tad late, but was accompanied by a smile, 'My, my! You really are a detective, aren't you? Well, I don't know for sure. I'm assuming a man can't stay so still that you wouldn't hear him all day through the famous walls of the luxurious Fairy Glen Resort and Convention Centre!'

Maity stared back at the man for some time, until the writer smiled again and said, 'You're looking at me as if I am hiding something, or who knows, as if I've had something to do with the murder of this woman!'

Maity smiled casually and said, 'I didn't say that.'

'You didn't say anything to the contrary either! But hey, I have read enough detective stories in my life to know that you have to suspect everyone. Therefore, I am a suspect too. I understand that. And I am not one of those people who will be offended by that. I mean, I know what I have and haven't done.'

Maity nodded, 'I appreciate that. Makes my job much easier. What can you tell me about this couple?'

Mr Subramaniam finished his omelette, wiped his lips with the napkin, glanced at the photograph of the honeymoon couple Kishore and Riya Rajbanshi, and shook his head. 'Never seen them. Were they staying in the hotel too?'

Maity completely avoided his question and asked, 'And finally, how about this man?'

I looked down to find a close-up of Harish Jhunjhunwala's chubby, sweaty face.

Mr Subramaniam shook his head again and said, 'Never seen him either. Sorry to disappoint you! I don't think I have been of much help to you, Mr Maity.'

Maity slid all the photographs back into the envelope, finished his coffee in one big gulp and said, 'You have no idea how much you have helped me! I wish you all the best with your novel. And if all goes according to my plan, there's a good chance we will meet again! Have a good evening ahead! Come, Prakash.'

As Sayantan and I followed Maity and stepped on to the footpath on Park Lane, I turned around one last time to look at the wall-to-wall glass facade of Café Columbus. Through it, through the design of the logo, through the floral patterns and the waves, I could see aspiring writer Mr T. Subramaniam looking at us with a fixed glance as he sat back in his chair and sipped on his chocolate milkshake. And I did not like that look. Not one bit.

[8]

The three of us came and stood in a relatively quiet corner of a by-lane, a little away from the main road. Maity seemed lost, and I didn't like seeing him this way. Usually in all the cases we have been on together, he tends to be in complete control of things, always working away at the puzzle in the centre of it all. But right now, he looked well and truly baffled. Sayantan seemed to be regretting bringing the case to Maity in the first place; there was a look of defeat and apology on his face. If only, if only this nitwit of a man had come to see Maity earlier, instead of sitting on the information for a whole week, perhaps we would have been able to nab the killer. Robert Sullivan had disappeared now, and there was no way to get to him. Not without involving the police, at least. I walked up to Maity, who was pacing up and down the lane like a caged tiger.

'Don't you think it's time we spoke to Satish, Maity?' I asked. 'The police will have enough tactics to arrest Bob Sullivan in Bangalore and bring him back here. It's their job.'

Maity was mumbling something; I couldn't quite catch what he was saying. Then he suddenly stopped and looked up at the building in front of him. We were facing the side of the building—the front façade was on the main road to our left.

'This is the Fairy Glen, isn't it?' Maity said.

I looked up at the building and realized he was right. Unknown to ourselves, we had come into the narrow lane between the hotel and Sayantan's building.

Maity mumbled something again, staring up at the room where Bob and Edith Sullivan had stayed.

'What?' I asked, trying to understand what he was saying.

'Why did they come and stay here?' Maity said.

I thought about it for a second. It was a valid question. The Sullivans' neighbour had said they were on their way to Bangalore. They would have either had to catch a train from Howrah station, which was closer to their home, or take a flight from the airport, which could be easily reached by cab. What were they doing in *this* hotel?

Maity had swivelled around and turned his attention to the other building, the one in which Sayantan Kundu lived. The young man was right. It was just a massive wall of red bricks rising into the sky. There wasn't a single window on this side of the building. No wonder some of the guests of the hotel didn't bother to draw their curtains.

Maity was squinting hard. I knew what he was looking for. But from where we stood, Sayantan Kundu's peephole was simply not visible.

Maity gave up and thought for a few seconds. Sayantan and I waited for him, patiently, almost helplessly.

'I think it's time to speak to Mr Brennan again,' Maity finally said and started walking towards the main road. 'There are a few questions that . . .'

As he trailed off, I signalled Sayantan to join us and followed Maity into the main road, turned right and walked through the main entrance of the hotel to reach the lobby, where Malcolm Brennan was standing behind the counter, reading a fashion magazine.

'Good afternoon!' Maity greeted the old man cheerfully, totally unfazed by the look of irritation on the latter's face on seeing him again. 'We are here again, like the proverbial bad penny, no less!'

'What do you want now?' said the man, grimacing.

'Tell me, Mr Brennan,' Maity was not one to give up so easily, 'when Robert Sullivan checked out, were you here at the reception?'

'I am always here at the reception,' grumbled the man. 'Who else will be here? Who else is left?'

'Do you remember the time when he checked out?'

'Early,' Brennan replied. 'Wee hours of the morn. Said they had a red-eye to catch.'

'They?' Maity asked, taking a step forward.

'He and his wife,' answered Malcolm Brennan.

'You saw his wife leave with him?'

'What kind of a question is that?' grimaced Malcolm Brennan. 'Yeah, of course I saw his wife leave with him! She seemed a little sick. The guy said she had had one too many to drink. But their rooms were paid for in advance. I asked them if they needed a receipt, he said that wouldn't be necessary. So I wished them well, and they were on their way.'

'So they had made a reservation in advance?'

'Yes, two nights. Check-in on the eighteenth, checkout on the twentieth.'

'Did he say where they were going?'

'Yeah!' said Malcolm Brennan. 'He said they were going to Bangalore. He seemed in a hurry though. Was probably late for his flight.'

Maity frowned, and I could immediately see why. The Sullivans lived in Howrah. Why would they come and stay in a hotel near Park Street for two nights in order to catch a flight to Bangalore? But more importantly, why would a man offer up the information of where he was headed after committing a murder?

'Mr Brennan,' Maity said, 'what I am about to ask you is of utmost importance. I implore you to think carefully, before you give me an answer.'

Brennan looked at Maity suspiciously and flipped his magazine shut. 'Okay?'

'Did you see, and I mean really *see,* with your own two eyes, Mrs Sullivan leave with her husband that night?'

Mr Brennan thought for a few seconds, then looked at our faces in turn and said, 'I don't know what you gentlemen want me to say, but yes! She left with her husband. She seemed to be running a fever though.'

'Fever?' Maity almost pounced on the old receptionist. 'What made you think so?'

'I mean, why else would her face be almost covered in a scarf, her head covered in a hat—that too a man's hat—and why would she be wearing a huge coat? I mean, this is June! I can barely step away from under this fan without breaking into a sweat. That poor woman looked pale and cold, even under all those layers of clothing. Must have been a fever!'

The three of us glanced at each other. I looked at the old man's confused face yet again. The glasses on his eyes had thick lenses, which didn't say much about his eyesight. The shade on the dim lamp standing on the left of the counter had probably not been cleaned or dusted in a decade.

Sayantan was right. Bob Sullivan did walk past the reception with his wife's corpse in his arms!

'Can you confirm a few other details for me, Mr Brennan?' Maity asked.

'Do I have a choice?' came the response.

'Do any of your guests play the violin?'

Maity's question may have seemed strange to Sayantan, as apparent from the look on his face, but I remembered T. Subramaniam had said that he had heard the sound of the violin being played from one of the rooms.

'Not that I know of!' the receptionist replied. 'If someone complained, I would have known. But no one did.'

'You get a lot of complaints here, from the guests, I mean? Must be hard on you,' Maity said in as gentle a voice as possible.

'Oh yes!' said the old man, removing his glasses and rubbing his eyes in exhaustion. 'It's an old building, people seem to forget that. The rent's cheap. Not my decision—I just man the reception counter and manage the place. I have been telling the owner to increase the rent, but he doesn't seem to care. And why should he? He's got several other businesses. Other hotels, too: one on Camac Street, another in Sealdah, just outside the station. If you keep the rent cheap, what kind of people do you think would come and stay in your hotel?'

'They cause a lot of ruckus, I suppose?'

'All the time!' The man suddenly seemed to find an interest in speaking to Maity. From having been friends with him for a long time now, I knew that there could be no one better than Janardan Maity in figuring out how to win over the confidence of another human being.

'You won't believe me, if I told you,' continued Malcolm Brennan, 'there are complaints every single day! Some of them I do something about, some of them I don't. It's . . . it's impossible for an old man like me to go knocking on doors all the time.'

'I couldn't agree more.'

'I check in the guests, check them out, handle the money, pay the bills—I mean, I don't have ten hands like that goddess of yours, no offence.'

'None taken, sir.'

'Why, just the other day,' the man went on, 'some old man complained that there were . . . you know . . . noises coming from the honeymoon suite on the third floor. I told the guest, it's a honeymoon suite, you silly fool! What do you expect?'

'Was it Robert Sullivan who had complained?' Maity asked.

'Oh no, no! That guy seemed like a quiet, sensible man. Never gave me any trouble. This was some other guest—room opposite to the honeymoon suite. Across the corridor.'

I realized Malcolm Brennan must be talking about a room that was not visible through Sayantan Kundu's camera. On the west side of the building.

'And then,' the old man was in a flow, as Maity listened patiently and with rapt attention, 'a week or so ago, an elderly lady checked into one of the rooms on the third floor, just beside the honeymoon suite. She complained of noises too. Said there was no way she would be able to sleep amidst all that ruckus next door. I didn't even talk to her! It's not my job to go around giving sex education lessons to people, is it? I offered to change her room to one on the first floor, but she said she didn't want to stay in this hotel a minute longer!

Not sure what she was expecting—you get what you pay for! I told her: Lady, this is not the Ritz! I cannot refund you, and she left in a huff. Good riddance, I tell you! Otherwise, she would have woken me up in the middle of the night.'

'This lady,' Maity said. 'Is her name Mrs Zorabian? Room 302?'

'That's her!' said Malcolm Brennan. 'Silly old hag!'

'Are there drunken brawls and such too?' Maity continued with his questions.

'Oh yes! Every other night, you'll see people stumbling and hobbling out—intoxicated. Either on their own, or on the shoulders of someone else.'

'So visitors are allowed in the room?' Maity asked.

'If we didn't allow visitors, half of the hotel's guests would not check in, in the first place!'

'You sleep in that room back there?' Maity asked, pointing to a door behind the man, marked with the words 'No Admission'.

'Sometimes,' said Brennan, 'if I'm too exhausted. Most nights, I take a nap in this chair itself. Yeah, I know that look of surprise on your face. I don't mind it, it's become a habit now. I've been doing this job for thirty years.'

'What about the other staff?'

'There's a maid who comes in the morning, leaves around six; she does all the cleaning and housekeeping stuff. There's a boy who runs errands, carries luggage and does other odd jobs like that. Twelve-year-old chap, but quite cheerful. Guests seem to like him—they say his eyes smile. We used to have a restaurant here at the hotel. Ophelia! A sight for sore eyes she was. Warm, cosy, air-conditioned. Majestic chandeliers, comfortable seating, a beautiful bar, a small stage. We used to have jazz recitals, you know? Best of the best! Those days are gone now. We had to close her down a few years ago.'

Maity gave the man a moment to control his emotions.

'Now, it's only me,' Malcolm Brennan looked around him like a painter looks at his undiscovered, unappreciated masterpiece—with love, hurt and a hint of sadness. 'Everyone's left. The guests demand food to be served in their rooms sometimes. Or drinks. The boy does that for them. There are quite a few shops and restaurants on the road outside. He earns a handsome tip, it seems. I've never asked. I can't afford to pay him anything. And the owner sure doesn't. Still, he seems to stick around. Probably has nowhere else to go. We do share a meal though, every night. That's about the only thing I can do for that lad.'

Maity paused for a few seconds and said, 'There seems to be a salesman who's been coming here? One Jayant Sinha?'

'Yeah!' The old man pulled himself out of his nostalgia with a heavy sigh. 'He's a regular. Good man. Talks a bit too much though! But I've never heard a complaint about him in all these months.'

'How long has he been coming?'

'Three–four months, I suppose. Comes on the sixteenth, leaves on the twenty-third. Like I said, he's a regular.'

Maity smiled, 'Any idea why he hasn't left yet this time?'

'What do you mean?' Brennan asked, adjusting his glasses.

'Well, he is still staying here, isn't he?'

'No! He checked out last night!'

Maity frowned, 'That's impossible!'

Malcolm Brennan scoffed a little: 'You don't seem to suggest you know *more* about my guests' check-in and check-out times than I do, now do you?'

Sayantan and I looked at each other. Just a few hours ago, we had seen Jayant Sinha's room through Sayantan's camera. We could see some of his stuff lying around the room. A blue shirt, a pair of slippers, a small red folder on his desk.

'When exactly did he check out?' asked Maity.

'Just after midnight!' came the response.

'What on earth is going on, Maity?' I asked, as he stepped away from the reception counter and sat down on one of the sofas in the lobby, his head buried in his hands.

'This case!' he said, almost in a whisper. 'It's not as simple as it had seemed in the beginning, Prakash! The twists and turns it's taking is something I have never seen before. This changes everything.'

After this, there was only one thing we could do, so we did that. Maity asked Mr Brennan if he could pay a visit to the room Jayant Sinha was staying in. I had expected the receptionist gentleman to grumble again, but surprisingly, he didn't. Perhaps he realized that there was something really serious and suspicious going on in his hotel. And he wanted to play along and be of as much help as he could.

This was the first time Maity and I met the bellboy. Brennan had given him the keys and he led us up the stairs. He was dressed in a cheap shirt, a pair of ill-fitting jeans that hung from his shoulders with the help of a pair of suspenders, and a small cap that said, 'Pilot'. Brennan's guests were right—the boy had a smiling and amiable face, with expressive eyes and a somewhat soothing demeanour.

'What's your name?' Maity asked the boy.

'You can call me "Chief",' the boy smiled. 'Everyone does!'

Maity smiled and asked, 'Do you go to school?'

'Nah!'

'Why?' Maity asked. 'A smart boy like you should be in school.'

The boy put the key in the keyhole on the door to Room 202 and said: 'People go to school so that no one can make a fool out of them. That doesn't seem to be working! I've spoken to some kids who go to school. I don't want to be like them.'

I looked at Maity. He was staring at the boy, a soft, affectionate smile playing on his lips.

'But there's so much to learn!' he said gently.

'You don't have to go to school to learn things,' the boy responded and entered the room.

Maity stepped into the room and asked, 'And what do you plan to do for money?'

'Work!' came the immediate response.

Maity smiled again and turned his attention to the room itself. It was just like the other rooms we had visited yesterday. Perhaps a little more neatly arranged. Indeed, there were a few things that Jayant Sinha had left behind. Maity glanced at them casually and then went and stood by the window.

'The guy sure seems to have left in a hurry,' said Sayantan.

'How much time does it take to pack a shirt, a folder and a pair of slippers into a suitcase?' the boy said, as he gathered the things. As he opened the folder, I saw that it was empty.

Maity turned around, walked up to Sayantan Kundu and said in a low but steely voice, 'That boy is smarter than you ever will be. Is it still not clear to you that Jayant Sinha has literally run away from this hotel in the middle of the night?'

'But why would he run away?' Sayantan asked. 'And why would he not take some of his stuff with him?'

'There are far more important questions than those, Mr Kundu,' said Maity, as he walked back to the window and stared outside. 'Far more important questions waiting to be answered.'

Sayantan looked at me, as did the young boy. I knew there were a hundred different things going on inside Maity's head right now. Conjectures, combinations, possibilities, hypotheses, facts. Things heard, seen, even smelt. From the familiar way his right forefinger was flicking around in the air, I knew he was trying to work things out, inching forward, then taking a step back—all in the pursuit of a baffling and intricate puzzle that had seemed like a simple affair to us merely a couple of days ago.

'Prakash!'

I heard Maity call my name. I went and stood beside him.

'I am going to ask you something,' he said, in a gentle voice. 'You think hard—really, really hard—before you answer my question. Can you do that, my friend?'

'Yes, Maity!' I said, preparing myself.

But after a long pause, Maity asked me a question that I was just not prepared for. It seemed so mysterious to me that for a second or two, I was quite taken aback.

'What do you see outside that window?'

There was absolute silence in the room. I was silent, Sayantan was silent, even the boy had perhaps realized by now that something was going on, and was standing in one corner, staring at our faces. From somewhere far away, perhaps from one of the many bars and restaurants lining the footpaths downstairs, the thump of electronic music was reaching our ears. Maity was standing tall, his arms folded behind his back, his face calm, his eyes narrowed but twinkling with some mysterious thought, some complicated calculation that was obviously going on inside that head of his. I followed his gaze and looked out of the window. And there was literally nothing to see outside other than one and just one thing.

'It's just a red brick wall, Maity,' I said. 'I don't see anything else.'

'Exactly, my friend!' Maity whispered. 'Exactly!'

I looked at Maity to find him nodding gently, his face grave and serious, his eyes shining. He whispered a few final words.

'Just a red brick wall!'

□□□

After we stepped out of the Fairy Glen, Maity became completely silent. Sayantan went back to his apartment, and after dropping me home, Maity went on his way, without even saying so much as goodbye to me. I was not unfamiliar with this behaviour of his, so, of course, I didn't mind. But for the life of me, I couldn't figure out what he may have seen from Jayant Sinha's window that suddenly made him go so quiet. There was absolutely nothing to see there! The glass on Sayantan's ventilator was naturally camouflaged to such an extent that despite our knowing that it existed, we couldn't see it!

Nothing else happened that night, except one thing— which I think is worth writing about.

I took a cold and refreshing shower, had a relaxed dinner and went to bed. As I lay in my bed, several thoughts came wandering to me, like floating clouds. For instance, the fact that Robert Sullivan and his wife had, for some mysterious reason, checked into the hotel two days before leaving for Bangalore. Had Maity been wrong all along then? Did Robert indeed plan his wife's murder? It was quite obvious from their neighbour's statements that they used to quarrel a lot at home as well. What if Robert had reached the limit of his patience and decided to take a drastic step?

Furthermore, why did Jayant Sinha run away all of a sudden? Even more mysterious was the fact that he had stayed longer than he normally did. Both Sayantan and the receptionist gentleman told us that the man used to function like clockwork. Why then did he overstay? And then when he did leave, why did he leave in such a hurry?

My phone suddenly rang, and I reached for it to find that Sayantan Kundu was calling. It was past eleven o'clock in the night, and I had no intention of speaking to him. But then, remembering that he had his camera still pointed at those six rooms, and wondering if he had seen something new, I answered his call.

'Hello?'

'Hello, Mr Ray? This is Sayantan here, Sayantan Kundu.'

'What is it, Mr Kundu?'

'Listen, I tried calling Mr Maity too, but he didn't respond.'

I was familiar enough with Maity's state of mind to know that he was nowhere near his phone right now.

'What's the matter?' I asked. 'Has something happened?'

'No,' said Sayantan, 'not exactly. But . . . you know . . . a sudden thought occurred to me.'

I clutched my hair, let out a sigh and said, 'What thought?'

'Well, you see, ever since I got back home, I have been thinking.'

'And what is it that you have been thinking?' I couldn't help let a significant amount of disappointment and irritation slip into my tone.

'Well, I asked myself a simple question.'

'What question?'

'Who among the guests did we meet *before* we went to the Fairy Glen today, only to find out that Jayant Sinha had fled?'

'And . . .?'

'Don't you see, Mr Ray? It was Mr Subramaniam—the writer. He was the only person whom we had met and spoken to about the murder *before* we went to the hotel to meet Jayant Sinha. What if the two of them are in this together? What if he tipped off Mr Sinha that we are looking for him?'

I couldn't believe what I had just heard. If anything, I realized that for the last one year, Sayantan Kundu would have been an extremely inefficient and downright foolish blackmailer. The fact that he had not been caught yet was itself a matter of great surprise to me. I realized Maity was absolutely right about him. The fellow was not only corrupt, he was an imbecile of the highest order.

'Mr Kundu?' I said, patiently.

'You do see what I am trying to say, right?'

'What time is it over there now?'

'It's . . . it's 11.20,' he said. Obviously, even my sarcasm wasn't comprehensible to him.

'Yes, it's quite late. And I don't know about you, but I have an early start tomorrow morning. Therefore, I would really appreciate it if you let me have a few hours of undisturbed sleep. And just so you could have your share of sound sleep too, may I remind you that we met Mr Subramaniam this afternoon, whereas Mr Sinha had checked out last night itself.'

For a few seconds, there was no response from the other side. I checked my phone, the call was still on. Then I heard Sayantan Kundu's voice again, 'Oh! Oh . . . y-yes, I hadn't thought of that. How silly of me, really! I'm . . . I'm sorry to disturb you. I was just . . . trying to . . .'

'No worries,' I felt bad for having been so harsh with him; he was clearly not a very intelligent young man. 'I suggest you stop worrying about the entire thing and try and get some sleep. Trust me, Maity will take care of everything. He always does.'

'Well, that's really reassuring to know,' Sayantan sounded relieved. 'All right then, goodnight!'

I wished the man goodnight, placed my phone back on the nightstand, turned the AC down by one degree and went to sleep.

The next morning, I woke up with a grimace to find Janardan Maity himself standing by the bed, hunched over my face, his firm hand placed on my shoulder.

'You?' I said, squinting my eyes. 'What's the matter? I wasn't expecting you so early!'

'Wake up, Prakash,' said Maity, still hunched over me. 'We need to leave now! Sayantan Kundu is dead!'

[9]

As we climbed the ancient stairs up to the floor on which Sayantan's dingy apartment was, my heart was overwrought with confusion, shock and even a hint of sadness. I had spoken to the man just a few hours ago! And I remembered having been unnecessarily harsh with him, and thinking that he was an imbecile, good for nothing. I deeply regretted all that right now as, with my heart thumping inside my chest, step by step, I followed Maity towards the young photographer's apartment, bypassing numerous policemen, other residents of the building and curious bystanders.

On the way here, Maity had explained to me that he had got a call from Senior Inspector Satish Mukherjee of Park Street Police Station early in the morning, saying that Maity's number was found on Sayantan Kundu's phone log. Maity had already given Satish an inkling that he was involved in a case at the Fairy Glen. Satish had then put two and two together and given him a call.

As we stepped into the apartment, I almost threw up. I remember there was a part of Sayantan's bed, towards the kitchen, which was particularly damp and dirty. Cigarette butts heaped in a mound, ash on the floor everywhere, dirty towels and underwear lying around here and there, a pillow on which I would never rest my head even if my life depended on it, used cups, plates, an overflowing dustbin—I could go on and on. Lying on his chest on this bed, with his face towards the wall, was the man I had spoken to not more than a few hours ago. The sheet on the bed was dirty, I had already seen that twice in the past. It was now soaked with blood. Sayantan's lifeless right hand was resting on the floor, his wrist bent and buried in the ash collected over months from the cigarettes he had smoked.

Maity stared at the body for a long time; it seemed to me his face had turned into stone. Satish Mukherjee was speaking to an elderly gentleman with a stethoscope around his neck. On seeing Maity, he shook the other man's hand and walked up to us.

'Would you mind telling me what's going on, Mr Maity?' he said.

'I'll tell you everything, Satish,' said Maity, his voice sounding like the rumble of the clouds just before a thunderstorm. 'But will you first tell me what happened here?'

'Neighbour found the door half open. Smelt something burning. Entered the room to find him like this. Apparently, he had put on a pan to boil a couple of eggs. That's when the killer must have entered.'

'Stabbed?' Maity asked.

'No,' said the Inspector, 'slit his throat. Right through the windpipe.'

I felt sick again. Maity was silent for a second or two.

Then he asked, 'Signs of struggle?'

'None. He must have been taken completely by surprise.'

I immediately recalled how surprised Sayantan had looked when we had come to visit him for the first time the other day. Maity and I exchanged glances, and Satish noticed us do so.

'I think it's only fair that I ask some questions of my own now,' he said. 'That camera over there in front of that window—I'm assuming you know what it was being used for?'

Maity pulled Satish Mukherjee aside and told him the entire thing in a nutshell but without omitting a single important detail. Despite being a writer, I myself would never have been able to summarize the entire case so well. While the two of them were speaking and Satish Mukherjee was asking Maity a few more questions, my eyes went towards the camera. I knew that I was not supposed to touch anything at the crime scene, but I still stepped forward, bent down and looked out of the window.

The view was obviously not as clear as the one through the lens of the camera, but I could still see the six rooms of the Fairy Glen. On the top floor, Room 301 (Harish Jhunjhunwala's room) was now occupied by a young man. The room that we called the vacant room in our diagram was occupied by two women—an elderly lady and a younger girl. Seemed like a mother–daughter duo. The honeymoon suite was still vacant.

On the lower floor, Mr Subramaniam was nowhere to be seen. I was just wondering where he was, when he stepped into the room from what seemed like the bathroom, scratched his cheek, poured almost half a bottle of water down his throat and sat down at his desk. Then he stared at a page for some time, picked up his pen and started writing. Perhaps the news of the incident next door had not reached him yet. The other two rooms on the floor were both vacant. The stuff that Jayant Sinha had left behind had already been removed by the boy yesterday.

'Dollhouse!'

I turned around with a start to find Maity standing next to me in a hunched position and watching the rooms out of the window.

'Looks just like a dollhouse, doesn't it?' he said.

'What the hell is going on, Maity?' I asked.

Maity stood back up, placed his hand gently on my back and said, 'I feel bad for the young chap, Prakash. He went down the dark path at the crossroads of life. Several of us make that mistake. And I yelled at him several times for having done so.'

I told him about the call last night. Maity shook his head in regret and said: 'They say death is the greatest redeemer. Whether we believe in that or not, one thing is true. It is only because Sayantan Kundu had the courage to walk up to my door and speak to me the other night that we will be able to apprehend a killer. Had he not come to me, kept the entire thing to himself, the killer would have gotten away scot-free.'

'You seem quite sure of yourself,' I now said, looking at Maity. 'Are you sure we will able to catch the killer?'

Janardan Maity looked at the crumpled-up corpse of the young photographer lying on the bed, and I saw his jaw turn stone-hard.

'I promise you, I will,' he said. 'That I promise you, my friend.'

In the next hour or so, several things happened. I will try to list them down one by one. This day had perhaps been the most eventful day since this dark and bizarre episode started, but as Maity spoke, I realized it had only begun.

First, Maity and I gave Senior Inspector Satish Mukherjee all the details that we had collected from the guest register of Hotel Fairy Glen.

Second, Maity suggested that Satish send his men to coordinate with the Bangalore Police to see if they could trace down a man named Robert Sullivan, although he added that thanks to the murder of Sayantan, he felt that the search would be fruitless. He added that Mukherjee could find more details such as copies of identity cards and address proof, etc., in the records of the Fairy Glen.

Third, Maity also suggested that the police bring Mr T. Subramaniam into the station for interrogation and see if he could shed some light on the second murder.

Fourth, Maity suggested that the Kolkata Police coordinate with the Kharagpur Police to look for a gentleman named Harish Jhunjhunwala. Apparently, that's where he was from. Maity also told Satish that he had a feeling Mr Jhunjhunwala was hiding from the law for reasons unknown.

Fifth, Maity said that he would go looking for Jayant Sinha himself. When asked why, he said he had a very good idea where he could be found and that since Mr Sinha did not know who Janardan Maity was, he would not see him coming. That would make things easier.

Finally, Maity turned to me and said, 'Prakash, here's Kishore Rajbanshi's address. I want you to go and meet both him and his wife. Will you manage to do that?'

I was completely unprepared for this, but I somehow pulled myself together and said yes. Satish Mukherjee looked at me suspiciously and asked, 'Will he be able to do it? Or should I send someone?'

'There's enough on your plate already,' said Maity. 'You and your men will take time to get to the couple. I am going for Sinha. Under the circumstances, it's best that Prakash goes. He will be able to leave right away. And all he has to do is to ask some questions in a non-threatening manner. He's been by my side long enough to know how to do that. What do you say, Prakash?'

'I'll go,' I said, feeling quite excited inside. 'I'll manage.'

'Excellent,' said Maity. 'Let's spread out, then.'

'Hang on a second, Mr Maity,' interjected Satish Mukherjee. 'If you don't mind, I have something to say to you.'

Maity sighed and turned around, even as I wondered what was going on. Satish stared at Maity for a while and said, 'You do realize what I am going to say, don't you?'

'I do, I do,' replied Maity.

'I don't have to tell you that I have the highest amount of respect for you and for your work. You know that, for a fact. But you made a grave error in judgement when you decided to keep this blackmailer fellow's activities close to your chest. When you chose to give me only half the information. I trusted you, so I played along. But that's a mistake *I* made. If only you would have taken me into confidence, if only you would have respected the law and let it take its course, then this man wouldn't be lying dead in this filthy room. We have laws and rules in a civilized society for a reason, Mr Maity. I am sure a man of your wisdom and experience needn't be told anything more than that.'

Maity nodded briefly. I have never seen someone speak to him like that, and my heart ached to see the sad and grave expression of regret on my dear friend's face. Satish Mukherjee turned around and walked away towards his men. Maity looked at me and gestured for me to be on my way. I was feeling so stifled and claustrophobic in that little room that I shot out of there and breathed a sigh of relief only when I had run down the stairs, walked past the crowd on Park Lane and reached Park Street. Never before in all the adventures I had gone on along with Janardan Maity had I felt so defeated. My mind was in a whirl, and my legs were trembling. I knew I had a job to do—my dear friend had entrusted me with a serious responsibility. So I calmed myself down, breathed in and out to fill my lungs with air and wiped the sweat off my forehead.

The address that Kishore Rajbanshi had written in the register of Hotel Fairy Glen was of a neighbourhood in Selimpur, near Dhakuria. I knew there was a slum in the area, and a quick look at Google Maps showed me that the address was right in the centre of that slum. I booked an Uber and found myself speeding towards the southern part of the city.

But as it turned out, when I reached the address bang in the middle of the slum, I realized that Kishore Rajbanshi didn't live there any more. His parents stepped out of their shanty hut and were quite surprised to know that I was looking for him. The father was dressed in a shabby kurta and a chequered lungi, had almost two weeks' grey beard on his face and a head full of unkempt, uncared-for grey hair. The mother was dressed in an equally shabby saree, and seemed much younger than her husband. There were signs of poverty all around me, and their shanty was no exception.

'What has he done now?' asked his father.

'Oh no, he hasn't done anything,' I tried to assure the elderly couple. 'I just wanted to speak to him and his wife.'

'His wife?'

We had to wait for a few seconds to continue the conversation, because a local train travelling towards Sealdah hurtled past us, setting the entire place—the shanty, the lamp post it was leaning against and myself—rattling to the core.

When the train had passed, it was the mother who spoke first, 'So he has married that girl?'

'You . . .' I hesitated, 'you didn't know?'

The poor old couple looked at each other, and the mother buried her face in the corner of her saree and broke down.

'We had asked him to stay away from that girl,' the father said. 'From what you are saying, it seems our words have fallen on deaf ears.'

I suddenly felt very helpless without Maity around. This was the first time I was doing this, and it was much more difficult than I had thought it would be. To speak to another human being and extract the information that you are looking for—who knew such a seemingly simple task could, actually, be *so* difficult? My respect for my friend grew several times at that very spot.

I was wondering what to say next, when the man himself asked, 'What business do you have with my son, sir?'

'I know him,' I said. 'From a few years ago, through a common friend.'

'You know his wife, too?' the man asked calmly. 'Through this common friend?'

I realized that I had grossly underestimated the elderly gentleman's intelligence. Just because someone was poor financially didn't mean that they were stupid and gullible too.

'I . . . I don't *know* her, have met her once.'

The man sighed. The woman was still weeping silently.

'It's a sin to be born poor in this country, you know?' the man said. 'Especially if you are from a lower caste. Those two stains—they are very tough, very stubborn. You can't wash them off easily. Look at me, standing here before you, at the end of my life, knowing fully well that you are lying. That my only child is in some sort of trouble. Will probably end up in jail. Or worse still, dead. You work hard all your life, try to make an honest living. Starve, sweat, bleed, digest insults and slurs, keep mum, hoping that someday your child will live a better life, because you yourself cannot.'

Another train hurtled past us, and as it did, I saw the pain in that old man's eyes. It took me a few seconds to see the decades of pain all accumulated in those eyes.

'But those two tags? How do you take them off? They come off only when your life comes off. Life, indeed! Every ten minutes a train passes through here. Every ten minutes I have the opportunity to tear those two tags off myself. Can you imagine the strength it takes to *not* succumb to that temptation, sir?'

I stared at the man in silence. His weeping wife had by now placed her head on her husband's arm.

'I had put my son in school,' the man continued. 'So that he could get out of this place and live a respectable life. It didn't even have to be as good as the one you live. But better than . . . this, at least. Was it too much to ask for?'

I hung my head, missing my dear friend badly. I knew he would have probably handled this much better than I was doing. But if there was one thing that I had learnt from Janardan Maity, it was that when someone was telling you their plight, the least you could do was have the courtesy to listen. Everything else could wait.

'It was the company he kept that ruined him,' the man continued. 'His friends. All of whom came from this . . . this hellhole! And it's not like I blame only them. My son was no angel himself. Some of the greatest people in the world— freedom fighters, artists, scientists, businessmen, political leaders—they have all risen from places like this, worse than this. My son is to be blamed too. If there is one thing I would like to tell you today, sir, with a heavy heart, no less, it is this: stay away from the company of my son. He, or his friends, cannot be of any good to anyone.'

The woman's frail body shook as she cried. I found myself in a decidedly uncomfortable and unpleasant situation. But I made a distinct effort to keep calm and focus on the job at hand.

'Um . . . I was wondering if you could give me this lady's address?' I tried to put in a few words.

'If you've met her, like you say you have,' the man said, 'then you know very well that she's no lady. Speak to her parents, if you don't believe me. You want her address, I'll give you her address. But please don't come back here ever again.'

As he wrapped his arm around his wife and gently took her inside the hut, I could hear the final words that the old man said that day, 'Our son is dead to us!'

The address that Kishore's father had given me was that of a place in Circus Avenue, near Beck Bagan. I once again booked an Uber and set off. I texted Maity about my whereabouts but received no response.

When I reached the address and rang the doorbell, an extremely fashionable lady answered the door. It was quite a far cry from the place I was coming from, so I was dumbfounded for a second. But when I informed the lady that I was looking for a Riya Rajbanshi, she welcomed me in, offered me a seat and said that her daughter's name was Riya—only Riya—and that she would greatly appreciate it if I addressed her by that name.

'It's her screen name, you see?' she said, smiling gently. 'I'm trying to get her used to that. Takes some doing. Kids these days, I tell you! Did Bruno give you this address?'

'Bruno?' I muttered.

The lady said, 'No? Oh wait, I see! You've seen the portfolio! Gosh, that was money well spent then! So, tell me, sir? What can I get you? Tea or coffee? Or perhaps something stronger?'

The realization that something was terribly wrong and that there was a nasty confusion happening somewhere had slowly begun to dawn on me.

'Good god!' the lady exclaimed. 'Why are you so stiff? Relax, please be comfortable. I don't bite!'

'You . . . must be?' I somehow managed to ask.

'I'm Riya's mother,' she flashed what can be best described as a charming smile. 'I had a screen name too, once. But those days are gone now. I was born a Chatterjee, if you must know. But you, sir, come across to me as a man who knows the benefits of discretion, so I'm sure you'll keep that bit of information to yourself. Look at me! Babbling away about myself! We are here to talk about my daughter, not me! Aren't we, Mr . . .?'

'Ray!'

'Oh!' exclaimed the lady. 'I'll call Riya and tell her that her film career is already off to a great start! Darling?'

The lady rose to her feet and walked through the door behind me. I was wondering if I should grab the opportunity and just leave, but then I asked myself what would Maity do under the circumstances? I knew there was a job to be done—two murders had been committed and I had to keep my nerves steady.

'And here he is!' the lady entered the room like a satellite enters an orbit—in other words, twirling.

Two other people entered the room with her: a young man and an even younger-looking girl. I had seen their photographs already, so I knew what their names were.

'This is Mr Ray,' said the lady. 'And this is my daughter, Riya. And her husband and co-star Kishore. That's his screen name too. It goes well with his image, don't you think?'

I had the distinct feeling that the two kids could see what the older lady had failed to—that I was not who she thought I was. They looked at each other and then stared at me, but before they could say anything, I summoned up all my courage and said, 'Ma'am, I would greatly appreciate it if I could speak to them alone.'

'Why, of course, of course!' the lady responded. 'That's the most . . . er . . . professional thing to do. Back in our days too, it used to be the same—Mommy doesn't need to be here, angel! Nothing's changed over the years, it seems.'

'Mom!' Riya called out to her mother in a rebuke.

'Sure, sure,' she said. 'I'm going, I'm going.'

As the lady exited the room, Kishore and Riya Rajbanshi turned towards me.

'If you don't want to spend the night in a jail cell, please sit down.'

To this day, I have absolutely no idea from where I got the courage to say those words, that too in a voice so chillingly calm and composed. But they did have the desired effect. The two kids looked at each other, crossed the length of the room and quietly sat down on a double sofa, making me realize that years of watching the world from over Janardan Maity's shoulders had had at least some impact on me.

[10]

Even in this tense moment, I could not help but admire the tastefully decorated sitting room of Mrs Chatterjee's home. It was quite evident from what she had told me so far that she had been a an actress of yesteryear. And that her daughter too had followed her footsteps. It did seem to me, however, that neither of them had been too successful. And yet, the room I now sat in was a picture of elegance and grace. There were a few Monets on the left wall—from his Les Nymphéas series. Tagore, Bankim and Nazrul lined the shelves on the right wall, as did dozens of British, Russian, American, French and German authors, poets and playwrights. There was an old gramophone in one corner, from which emerged the faint but familiar sound of the Ricardos singing 'Cuban Pete'. The coffee table in front of me had quite a few magazines and newspapers strewn on it—a couple of *Vogues*, a few *Verves* and today's *Statesman* were among them. There was a framed image of Swami Vivekananda on the wall too, clad in saffron, back straight as an arrow, hands folded at the chest. From the frame hung a garland of stale marigolds. On the opposite wall, there was a framed black-and-white photograph of a ravishing young woman with one of the most beautiful smiles I had ever seen. It was a photograph of a young Mrs Chatterjee.

'We don't want any trouble,' Riya was the first to speak.

I noticed her more closely this time. She was dressed less fashionably than her mother, but I had to admit there was an elegant beauty in her simplicity. Other than perhaps the blonde dye that looked a tad tacky, she was clad in a beautiful frilly frock with rhomboidal patterns of blues and whites. Her eyes were large and lined with just the right amount of kohl, and right now it was obvious that she was wearing more make-up than what I had seen of her in the photographs. The other, more important difference between how she looked in those photographs and how she looked now was in her expressions. In the photos, her face wore a look of amorous feminine passion. Right now, all I could see in those eyes was fear.

'Nor do I,' I said, maintaining a calm but stern disposition.

'Who are you?' she asked. 'What do you want from us?'

I went straight to the point. 'On the nineteenth of this month, it was a Tuesday, you were staying at Hotel Fairy Glen on Park Lane, am I correct?'

The couple exchanged glances. Then the husband opened his mouth for the first time, 'Yes, but we are married—legally married. We didn't commit any crime.'

I shook my head and said, 'I never said you did, did I? But there has been an incident at the hotel, in the room right below yours, on that very night—nineteenth of June. A lady was murdered by her husband.'

Riya jumped up from her seat and almost yelled out: 'I knew it! I just knew it!' She turned to her husband and said,

'And I told you too! I told you there was something wrong. You didn't trust me. Do you see now?'

'What do you mean I didn't trust you?' the husband protested. 'We checked out as soon as we could, didn't we?'

'That's because I insisted. I literally had to drag you out of that hotel. And Ki, we've done three films together. Is that the kind of place you take your bride to on your honeymoon? The entire place reeked wrong. From the moment I stepped foot in that building, it gave me the creeps. You could have told me, honey, it's not like we can't afford a better hotel.'

'I don't want your money!' The man sounded hurt. It was obvious to me that his masculine pride had just been attacked.

'Goodness gracious, Ki!' The woman spread her hands and shrugged her shoulders. 'How many times have I told you that what's mine is yours too. What do you want me to do? Write that on some legal paper and sign below it? I mean, come on! We talked about this!'

'Hey, hey, hey!' I had to jump right into the arena where this domestic squabble had begun to develop. 'You can discuss all of that later, you have your entire life ahead to do that. Right now, I want to ask you a few questions regarding your stay there. So, please. Sit down, and more importantly, calm down.'

Kishore gestured to Riya and she sat down a little distance away from her husband. She was still sulking in a fit of feminine temper.

'Look, sir,' said Kishore, 'we don't want to cause any kind of trouble, okay? We'll cooperate in any way we can. But first, I want to ask you something.'

'Go ahead,' I nodded.

'How did you get this address?' he asked. 'This is not the address I had given to the hotel.'

'I went to the address you had given to the hotel,' I said calmly.

There was a long silence in the room, during which Kishore slowly hung his head. From the other end of the sofa, Riya looked at her husband. Somewhere hidden deep within that look, covered beneath the deliberate sheaths of annoyance, I could also see a hint of concern. Sitting there, in that room, I couldn't help but experience a range of emotions swirling in my heart. For the young man, his young bride, the bride's mother and the young man's parents. What a strange tapestry life had woven, I thought!

'How are they?' Kishore asked, softly.

I wondered what to say. Then I remembered what Maity had once told me—that a lie told to bring peace to someone's heart is way better than a thousand truths. I chose my words carefully and said, 'They are fine. They've moved on.'

Kishore nodded his head and sighed. 'Good!' he said. 'That's good!'

I said, 'Look, guys, I just want to ask you both a few questions. And then I'll be out of here.'

Kishore sniffed once and looked at me. 'Ask us what you want to know. We'll try our best to help.'

'Excellent! First, let's get some quick details out of the way. You checked in to the Fairy Glen on Tuesday, the nineteenth of June?'

'That's right. That's also the day we got married. Legally, that is. My mother-in-law is planning a small get-together early next month. On Tuesday, we left home early. The court opens at ten, but there was a long queue, and the registrar came almost an hour late. By the time we reached the registrar, it was almost half past one. I was afraid they may say it's lunchtime now, come later. That would have delayed things even further.'

'And all that heat!' quipped Riya.

'Yeah, it was messy. No fans, far too few benches for the kind of traffic the place gets. But at least we reached the desk before they announced lunch hour. I had a cab standing by, we had lunch in a restaurant. Fancy place, I'd made a reservation.'

I cast a quick glance at Riya to watch her reaction: she rolled her eyes and made a face that silently contested the veracity of her husband's claim about the restaurant he had taken her to.

'After that,' Kishore continued, 'the same cab brought us to the hotel at around half past four.'

'I'm assuming you had made a reservation at the hotel?' I asked.

'Oh yeah!' said Kishore, with a subtle hint of pride in his voice. 'The honeymoon suite was reserved for us, for three nights!'

'But you checked out the next morning itself?' I asked.

'Let me tell you the rest, sir,' Riya suddenly jumped into the conversation, much to her husband's visible dismay and discomfort. 'What does a woman want from her honeymoon, sir? You tell me?'

'I . . . I don't have the faintest . . . '

'A romantic destination, a glass of wine, some floral arrangements, a hotel with a pool, maybe a spa? A sunny beach, or the cosy hills. Goa or Gangtok. At least Digha, for Christ's sake. But no! My beloved husband decides to *surprise* me. How? By taking me to Park Lane! Fairy Glen, my foot! Not a single wall in that room is without a stain, I tell you. There's a little boy running around . . . I immediately asked him to change all the sheets and give us a fresh set of towels. Who knows who did what in that room before us?'

'About the check-out . . .?' I somehow managed to put in a few words.

'I'm coming to that. The heat was killing me! Government offices in this country—you know how they are. I took a long shower. Then came back into the room to find that my Prince Charming had fallen asleep!'

'Oh, for heaven's sake, Riya,' protested the husband. 'I was sitting on the bed with my eyes shut! I had been up at the crack of dawn.'

'I know you had been up at the crack of dawn, Ki,' said Riya, in a sing-song voice. 'Because guess who else was up at the crack of dawn? Guess who had to put on a ton of make-up and a gown that weighs twenty-five kilos before going to a filthy, paan-stained government office with family-planning posters covering half the wall? This girl!' she finished by pointing towards herself with both her thumbs. Then she turned towards me and carried on her commentary.

'He has this habit of falling asleep in the weirdest of places, you know? Why, just before you came, he was sleeping! But anyway, so we check in, then . . . you know . . . we spend some time together, we talk, we order some drinks. There's no room service, by the way. That's another . . . thing. Remember the little boy I told you about, who changed the sheets?

Yeah, he's the one running around doing all this. I think he does the cleaning too. Anyway, we have a few drinks, and then . . . you know . . . we retire for the night.'

'I see!'

'Yeah, the next day, we were supposed to meet my mom at Trinca's. My dad lives on Mission Row, he had also promised to come. He hadn't met Ki yet. But we had to cancel all the plans.'

'Why?'

'Because that night, I woke up on hearing some sort of noise. I am anyways a light sleeper, you see? But this noise was like . . . like really loud. Someone was yelling at the top of her voice. Yes, a woman. Middle of the night. Dogs started barking on the road outside. My husband was fast asleep, as always. I perked up my ears and listened carefully. It was some woman—she seemed to be shouting at a man, even the man was yelling back at her. They seemed like a couple. Only couples shout at each other like that.'

'Could you hear what they were saying?' I asked.

'Oh, vaguely. The woman was saying something about the man ruining her life, the man too was going on about her nagging all day. And . . . and . . . the fact that she couldn't give him a child. And I was like—what the heck, man? How do you know it's her fault? It could be you! I've read that in a . . . in a . . . in a magazine. And whatever it is—his fault, her fault—it doesn't matter! You don't get to say such a thing to your wife!'

'What happened then?' I asked.

'My husband has this annoying habit of snoring, you see? So I could barely hear what they were fighting about. And then I suddenly remembered this old movie I had seen, I can't remember the name, I think it had that sexy hero in it, what's his name, and that other pale-looking girl too. Anyway, I quickly went to the bathroom and there was a glass there next to the mirror. You know, like an ordinary drinking glass, except you don't drink from it. You use it to keep your . . . stuff. Toothbrushes and such. I did a smart thing with that glass. I brought it back into the room and turned it over . . . like this . . . and placed it on the floor. Then I placed my ear on the other end, and the voice became clearer. It was like a . . . like a telephone, you see what I mean?'

'That was most . . . ingenious of you,' I said patiently. 'And what did you hear?'

'Well, the couple were still quarrelling. And then I heard the woman let out a . . . a . . . little cry of sorts, you know. I could've sworn the man hit her. I mean . . . I've seen men hit women . . .'

Riya Rajbanshi seemed lost in her thoughts for a second or two, but she quickly pulled herself together and resumed her story: 'So anyway, I was quite sure the husband hit his wife. I heard the poor woman sobbing bitterly, and I heard the door slam. The wife continued to sob for a long time.'

'I see,' I said, turning my attention to the young man. 'And what were you doing all this while?'

Kishore Rajbanshi was taken aback for a second. Then he said, 'She . . . she woke me up and made me listen to the woman sobbing. Through that glass thingy. I asked her what was wrong. And she told me everything that had happened.'

'So, let me get this straight,' I said. 'The two of you heard a man and a woman quarrelling in the room below yours. You also claim that you heard the man hitting the woman, although there was no way for you to be sure of that fact. And this made you check out of the hotel the very next morning?'

The couple once again exchanged looks. Then Riya asked her husband, 'Will you tell him, or should I?'

'You tell him,' he said.

'Mr Ray,' Riya dragged herself forward to the edge of her seat, 'there's more! I'm not quite sure about this, but later that night, I mean, after we had fallen asleep and all, I think I heard the muffled screams of the woman from the room below. I think I also heard some kind of masculine grunts. Like I told you, I am a light sleeper. And Ki was sleeping on his side, so his snoring had also come down. But I thought that's what I heard. As if . . . as if the man was trying to kill the woman somehow, by strangling her to death or something, or choking her with his bare hands. And I immediately woke him up, as silently as I could. And I told him what I had heard, in whispers. We couldn't sleep the rest of the night. He double-checked the lock on the door, and we lay quiet in our beds, wondering if we had made any sound which could have been heard in the room downstairs. I mean, think about it. If we could hear the killer, then the killer could hear us too, right? That's only logical.'

'Precisely!' I nodded.

'Well, Ki dozed off again, and this time, I once again did something smart. I let him snore. Didn't wake him up or push him on to his side. If the killer would be listening, then he would at least know that the people upstairs were fast asleep, having not heard anything. But I was wide awake, my senses heightened—waiting to hear even the slightest sound. Late at night, at around 2 a.m. or so, I heard the door of the room downstairs open, someone flicked a switch and the door closed. And then, nothing.'

'You are sure of the time?' I asked.

'Absolutely sure,' said Riya. 'It was exactly 2.24 a.m. when the man left the room. I checked my phone.'

'Why didn't you wake me up?' said Kishore.

'To do what?' Riya flared up in an instant, 'As if you would have gone out and confronted the killer, eh? Kung fu-ed him to hell?'

'At least . . . at least I could have done something,' the husband protested. 'Called the cops or something.'

'Ki, I'm telling you, honey, don't make me angry—'

I was unwilling to witness yet another exhibition of marital discord, so I quickly rose to my feet, thanked them, wished them a happy married life and told them that if required, they may be summoned to the police station for further questioning. When they seemed concerned about that last prospect, I told them what Maity usually tells all his suspects: 'There's nothing to be afraid of. If you've not done anything wrong, then you don't have anything to worry about.'

Having said this much, I left the room. No sooner had I set foot on the road outside, I heard the mother enter the room. 'So he's not a film-maker?' I heard her say in an angry voice, and I almost ran out of the lane.

The job that Maity had given me was done. It was now time to go back and report my findings to him. The newly-wed couple Kishore and Riya Rajbanshi were probably the only witnesses to the murder of Mrs Edith Sullivan by her husband Mr Robert Sullivan. The biggest problem was that they were not eyewitnesses. The one and only eyewitness to the murder of Edith Sullivan was dead.

[11]

The part of the city where I now stood after coming out of Mrs Chatterjee's home was largely populated by Muslims. But one or two houses here and there had Anglo-Indian residents as well. This was south of Park Street, and the signs of our former rulers were strewn about and visible here and there. In the past, this used to be a busy street, so busy in fact that the authorities decided to build a massive flyover on top of it—one that started at the eastern fringes of the city, bypassed all the traffic signals and took one all the way down to the Victoria Memorial. While that may have offered a lot of convenience for the commuters who used this street regularly to get to the financial district of the city, it had given the once-vibrant street a rather bleak and gloomy look. I knew this because I had seen the street both before and after the flyover was built. I looked around, and a general sense of sadness enveloped me. I figured time was passing by far sooner than what I was able to cope with. The city was changing. Perhaps for the better. Or maybe for the worse. Who knew? If this was progress, at what cost had it been achieved?

I gave my thoughts a moment and then pulled myself together. Although my assignment was over and done with, the overall job was yet to be done. I had to get back to Maity and report what I had found out. Maity always insisted on hearing the little details, because he said that sometimes, a seemingly inconsequential and insignificant detail was exactly where the key to the entire puzzle was hidden. Relaying to Maity everything I had seen, heard and felt would be quite a job in itself. I pulled out my phone to find that I had received a text in response to the one I had sent Maity a couple of hours ago. I stood on the footpath in front of a restaurant and stared at the message for a long time but couldn't make head nor tail of it. The content of the message was as mysterious as the sender himself. It read: 'CTC 1400. Place Jewel Thief. Take S14R5.'

Trust Janardan Maity to make things complicated for no reason at all! The man's love for puzzles could get irritating sometimes. I was feeling hungry—hadn't had time to have anything for breakfast, hadn't even had a cup of coffee throughout the day. Moreover, the shock of seeing Sayantan Kundu's mutilated corpse—it was all getting to me. And a puzzle to solve was literally the last thing I wanted right now! I made up my mind. First things first, I had to eat. Otherwise, I would simply faint. I turned around to look at the restaurant; it turned out to be a relatively well-known place in Park Circus. I stepped in and asked for a table, and was immediately ushered to a place in a corner. The owner of the restaurant clearly didn't give too much importance to décor. It was not a shabby ambience; in fact, the entire place bore a neat and clean look. But it wasn't what I would call a comfortably fancy place either. Maity, however, often said that some of the best food in a city like Kolkata could be found in some of the most ordinary eateries. Maity wasn't the sort of man to pay any attention to ambience.

The waiter greeted me warmly, poured me a glass of water and came back to take my order. I hadn't even looked at the menu by then; I was still looking at the bizarre message on my phone.

'What's good here?' I asked the waiter, without even looking at him.

'You should try our special mutton biryani, sir,' he said. 'We make it with authentic—'

I cut him off and asked him to get me a plate of mutton biryani along with a can of Coke.

'May I suggest something, sir?' the waiter said. 'It is a chilled bottle of Thums Up that will go better with the biryani. That too, not just any Thums Up—but a Thums Up in a cold glass bottle! Not a plastic one. Some people say, Coke, Pepsi, Thums Up, what difference does it make? But trust me when I tell you sir, it does!'

I am well aware that there are some people who genuinely love to talk. They can just break out into a conversation with even a perfect stranger, go on and on, and just don't know when to shut up. I realized the waiter fellow was just that sort of a guy, and truth be told, I hate such people. They get on my nerves. I myself speak very little, and only when it is absolutely necessary. I like to be left in peace in my own private space—undisturbed, unbothered. I had already had a bad day and was almost about to lose my patience with this gabby old chap, but I somehow controlled myself. I looked up at the waiter. He was roughly my age, had a fittingly foolish grin plastered on his face and was probably busy changing my preference of drink on his order book without even having taken my permission to do so.

This had to be dealt with, I thought. That too, sternly.

'Your name is Nalin?' I asked, looking at his tag. He was clad in a white shirt, a crimson waistcoat and a pair of black trousers. The typical waiter's uniform in this part of the world. His hair was arranged with great perfection, and he sported a butterfly moustache under his nose.

'Yes, sir!' The foolish grin expanded to become downright irritating. 'Nalin Shukla! I've been in the hospitality industry for—'

'Mr Shukla,' I said in a serious, steely voice. 'I am already quite disturbed since the morning. I would greatly appreciate it if you brought me a can of Coke, and not a Thums Up. Had I wanted a chilled bottle of Thums Up, I would have taken care to see that I communicated that to you in clear, unambiguous words. Since I haven't asked for a chilled bottle of Thums Up, and since I have asked for a chilled can of Coke instead, and since you have clearly heard me request the latter—because otherwise you would not have taken the trouble to suggest an alternative that *you* think I would prefer—would you be so kind as to get me the drink I chose to order along with my food, so that I can have my fill in peace, pay this establishment for my meal and be on my way?'

The grin had vanished altogether and the man bit his tongue and said in an apologetic voice of concern, 'I can see Dada is very hungry, no?'

'Mr Shukla!' I shut my eyes and raised my voice by a decibel. I was now standing at the edge of my patience.

'Ten minutes, Dada.' The man snapped his order book shut and almost ran away from the table. 'Just ten minutes!'

I, on the other hand, placed my phone on the table, took a sip of the water and pressed my palms on my eyes. The air-conditioning was cooling me down, but my head had become hot and heavy, and my heart was racing. Everything was happening so fast! There was so much information to process! Sayantan's shocking murder! And then running around the city looking for the honeymoon couple. And finally, the two bizarre and contrasting experiences with the couple's parents. I realized it had all become too much for me, and that more than anything else, I needed a moment to just calm down.

I went to the washroom and splashed a lot of cold water on my face. That seemed to help. I looked at myself in the mirror. I hadn't shaved that morning and wore a haggard look. My eyes were bloodshot and I looked exhausted. I stood there for a few seconds wondering how wrong I had been to have thought that the case was too simple for Janardan Maity to take on. Maity often said that puzzles could be deceptively difficult to solve. One might even consider not attempting a seemingly simple puzzle, when, in reality, it would be an astonishingly tough one to crack. This case turned out to be just that sort of a puzzle. I wondered if the Bangalore Police would be able to apprehend Robert Sullivan simply on the basis of his name and date of birth. I knew Satish and his team would start with flight records, but after that, how the local police over there would act—I had absolutely no idea.

I came back to my table only to find that the food had not yet arrived. I shook my head in frustration, let out a deep sigh and sat down. I opened Maity's cryptic message again and focused on it:

CTC 1400. Place Jewel Thief. Take S14R5.

The abbreviation in the first part of the message probably meant 'cost to company'—like when a salary is offered to a job applicant. But what job would pay Rs 1400 per month? Several, I suppose, although it did seem to me that it would be extremely difficult to get by on that sort of an income. Perhaps it was a weekly income, then? But why was Maity telling me about a job? I gave up and moved on to the second part of the message, which seemed even more mysterious than the first. Jewel thief? What jewel was Maity referring to? Was there a jewel involved in this story somehow? And how or when was it stolen? And who stole it? Who was the jewel thief? I remember Maity had said that he knew where he would find Jayant Sinha. Did he suspect Jayant Sinha of the theft of some mysterious jewel that I had failed to see in the photographs then? And what on earth did he mean by 'place jewel thief'? Place jewel thief . . . what . . . under arrest? How on earth was I supposed to do that?

Then it suddenly occurred to me that perhaps Jewel Thief was the name of a place he was referring to. Perhaps a restaurant or a café somewhere—I hadn't noticed the uppercase 'J' and 'T' so far. But if he had given me a place where I was supposed to meet him, then shouldn't he have mentioned a time too?

It suddenly struck me like a flash of lightning that he had, in fact, done so! 1400 was no salary. It was a time! Maity was asking me to meet him some place called Jewel Thief at 2 p.m. I quickly googled the name of the place but other than posters and scenes from the movie of the same name, I couldn't find anything. Then I searched for 'Jewel Thief restaurant' and yet again, nothing. Jewel of the Nile—yes. The Crown Jewel—yes. Even Kohinoor—sure. But no Jewel Thief. I wasn't giving up so easily. This time, I changed my search string to 'Jewel Thief Café', although why someone would name their café in so odd a fashion was alien to me. I was just about to give up when, on the second page of the search results, I found an entry that drew my attention. It said 'Jewel Thief Entertainment', and I clicked on the link to find that it was an escape room! I knew these escape rooms had now become a fad with youngsters, and several of them had cropped up around the city. They lock you and a few others in a room and give you a fictitious situation. And you have to escape the room before a timer runs out. For instance, they may put you in a library whose doors and windows are all locked from the outside. They may say someone has planted a time bomb in the room and it is ticking. You would then have to find clues from all around the room and figure out a way to get out before the timer runs out and the bomb explodes. Figuratively, of course.

It all became clear to me now. CTC was not 'cost to company', it meant Calcutta Tramways Company. They also ran buses. Maity wanted me to take the 2 p.m. CTC bus and reach this Jewel Thief escape room place. Exactly the sort of place that a puzzle lover like Maity would want to go to. I had already learnt that it was near Ruby Hospital, on the Eastern Metropolitan Bypass. But 2 p.m. CTC bus from where?

I realized that was where the S14R5 thing came into the picture. I was quite sure it was some sort of a route number or something, and I just had to look it up on the Internet. I was almost about to do so when the smell of fresh mutton biryani hit my nose and set my stomach rumbling and my mouth watering.

The waiter had hurriedly brought my plates and cutlery, and just behind him, another young chap dressed in the same uniform was carrying the plate from which the aroma was wafting around.

'There you are, Dada,' said the waiter, 'your food is here. And very sorry, I . . . I didn't mean to . . . disturb you earlier . . .'

I smiled politely and shook my head.

'Here's your mutton biryani, I have asked the kitchen to put two extra aloo in it. And here's your Coke! Shall I pour it in the glass for you?' The young man had bent down from the waist to stare right into my face.

'No, thank you!' I said, hoping that he would not make the same mistake again and just leave me to myself, so that I could enjoy my food in peace.

The waiter brought his hands together in a clap with a look of satisfaction and excitement on his face and said: 'Well then, please enjoy your meal. If you need me just raise your hand and signal. I'll keep an eye on you.'

I ignored the verbal volley of the man and picked up my fork without saying anything.

'And, of course, good luck with the race!'

I looked up to find Nalin Shukla walking away hurriedly towards the other end of the restaurant, wiping his forehead with a handkerchief, even though the air conditioner was running full blast.

I kept staring at his retreating figure. What did he mean by those last words?

'Excuse me!' I raised both my hand and my voice. Shukla had heard me and was now dashing back to me with a look on his face that portrayed sheer fear. He perhaps thought that there was something wrong with my food.

'Yes, Dada?' he said, still sweating profusely. 'Did they not give the extra potatoes?'

'What did you just say?' I asked, frowning.

'What did I just . . .' the young man took a step back and shook his head. 'Oh no, no! Please don't get me wrong. When

I said I'll keep an eye on you, I meant I'll . . . you know . . . just keep watching if you need anything . . . I'll . . . just be alert. That's what I meant. Just a way of saying. Please don't take it otherwise, Dada.'

'No, no, Mr Shukla, you said: "Good luck with the race!" What race?'

Nalin Shukla paused for a second, 'Oh that! I mean, how silly of me! You know, my father tells me I talk too much. Why, even the manager here . . . he'll kill me if he . . . I thought you were going to the race. Weren't you? I'm *so* sorry, Dada! I shouldn't have peeped at your phone. It's rude, and unprofessional, and an unquestionable violation of your privacy. Moreover, I shouldn't assume things about people. That's just . . . wrong!'

I looked down at the message Maity had sent me and said, 'This message? You are talking about this message?'

'Y-yes!' He was still apologizing profusely for his behaviour and his words. 'I made a mistake, and I sincerely apologize. I hope you won't mind.'

'No, Mr Shukla,' I said. 'Hang on, hang on for a second. You know what this message means?'

'Why, yes Dada!' he said. 'CTC obviously refers to the Royal Calcutta Turf Club. 1400 probably means 2 p.m., I mean that's when the race starts today.'

'Race?' I asked, flabbergasted, 'What race?'

'Why, horse race, of course! The one you bet on?'

I looked up at him in absolute awe. 'And . . . and the rest?'

'The rest is simple,' he said. 'Jewel Thief is the name of a horse, it's had a few good runs lately; the jockey is also an experienced young man. Place Jewel Thief means put a

"Place" bet on Jewel Thief. Which means your horse, which is Jewel Thief, has to finish first, second or third for you to win. And S14R5 obviously means the place in the stands where you will be sitting. Section 14, Row 5. But you obviously knew all that, Dada! Look at me, blabbering away once again! But I . . . I do have a sincere request to make to you, Dada.'

I stared blankly at the man's face, my biryani lying on my plate, my hunger forgotten.

'You see, although I have been in the hospitality industry for a long time, my job here is new.' He took a step forward, lowered his voice and pleaded with me, 'Please don't complain to the manager. Or write a bad review online. I . . . I just can't seem to control this nasty habit of mine. Whenever I meet people I just . . . I just feel like talking to them . . . you know?'

I couldn't take it any more. I jumped up on my feet and hugged the man. Several heads turned towards my table. Everyone looked at what was happening with curiosity and surprise, and when I let go of Nalin Shukla, he looked the most baffled.

'I can't thank you enough, Mr Shukla,' I said. 'You have no idea what a big hassle you have saved me from. I would have gone in the completely opposite direction.'

'Oh!' The man's grin had returned to his face, and this time, when I looked at it, it seemed genial, not foolish. 'Well, I'm glad to be of some help, Dada!'

I sat back down at my table, looked at the entire message again and nodded my head. Then I looked up at the waiter and said, 'Can I tell you something, Mr Shukla? Don't ever change, please. And don't let anyone tell you that you need to stop talking to people. You have a gift! A genuine gift that most of us simply don't. I am sorry I shouted at you, I really am. You were right, and I was wrong. Please, don't ever change.'

The young man smiled and said, 'Oh! That's very kind of you to say, Dada!'

'And one more thing,' I said. 'You can take this Coke away and get me a Thums Up!'

Nalin Shukla grinned from ear to ear, picked the can of Coke off the table, and said with an amiable shake of his head, 'Excellent choice, Dada! Kolkata biryani tastes *best* with a chilled bottle of Thums Up! And not just any bottle!'

'A glass bottle!' I said, as the man nodded with a smile and walked away to get me my drink.

[12]

I had never set foot inside the Royal Calcutta Turf Club. I had only seen it from the outside in all the years that I had lived in Kolkata, nor had I ever witnessed a single horse race. I found that quite strange, now that I thought about it, as I entered through the gates of the racecourse and made my way through the crowd to the ticket house. I told the gentleman at the counter that I was new to betting, but that I had been advised by a friend to put a 'Place' bet on Jewel Thief. The man behind the counter was at least sixty, if not more, had a weary and exhausted look on his face, was clad in a shabby kurta and a shabbier dhoti, and the ancient table fan running full speed right next to his face made his voice sound mechanical—as if it was coming out of a robot or an android of some sort. He asked me how much I wanted to bet, scribbled something on a small booklet hastily with a piece of lead pencil in his hand, tore off the ticket, stuffed it in my palm and said, 'If there is one piece of advice that I can give you about gambling, it is that you should never, ever listen to anyone else's advice. Next!'

I came out of the queue and looked at my watch: 1.40 p.m. The race was about to begin, announcements were being made over loudspeakers. The place wasn't as busy as I had thought it would be. Maity later told me that there was a time when horse races were one of the greatest attractions of the city, but that over time, this form of entertainment had lost most of its charm. Now, mostly gambling addicts came to the races, whereas earlier, the upper echelons of the city's social classes were regularly seen in the club. I looked at the clubhouse itself. It was a majestic building to say the least. But like most other British-era buildings in the city, it now showed signs of decay, dismay and neglect.

I looked around to check if I could see Maity anywhere, but couldn't find him in the crowd. It seemed to me that bit by bit, the crowd was also swelling. A long queue had formed at the betting counters. Announcements were being made more frequently. Security guards in khaki were blowing their whistles and waving their batons to control the crowd. People from all walks of life were visible in the crowd, mostly men—although I did catch the glimpse of quite a few women too, especially in the seats in the upper stands, lining the veranda of the actual clubhouse. Those seats were probably for regular members of the club. I had heard that there was a beautiful restaurant inside the club too, open only to members. I was looking around at the crowd and wondering if Maity was there somewhere, or if I should call him, when my heart suddenly stopped in an instant.

A beige-coloured Havana hat with a black band was floating on the ocean of bobbing heads. Under the Havana hat, and visible to me only every now and then, was a thick neck and a broad pair of shoulders. And adorning those shoulders was a blue-coloured shirt. I had seen this shirt very recently—hanging from the wall of Room 202 at Hotel Fairy Glen.

Jayant Sinha!

I suddenly started to feel uncomfortably warm and sweaty. My legs too felt weak. It was one thing to pursue and speak to a harmless couple. But this man somehow seemed dangerous to me. I remember he had fled from the hotel—for what reason I don't know. Nor did Maity. Why had he sent me here? And didn't he say that he was on Jayant Sinha's tail? Did that mean he was here somewhere, watching? But where? I couldn't see him anywhere.

The Havana hat disappeared behind a row of pillars and appeared after a couple of seconds, accompanied by a thin swirl of smoke. I realized Jayant Sinha had stopped to light a cigarette. My eyes followed the hat, my body taut and alert. The crowd had really started swelling now. The sun had started dipping behind the clock tower towards the west. My feet felt like they were glued to the ground. Amidst all this, I saw Sinha come and stop under a sign that said 'No Smoking'. He looked up at the sign, frowned heavily and then threw his cigarette on the ground. And at that exact moment, something or someone touched me near my thigh and startled me for an instant, before I realized it was my phone and that it was vibrating. I opened it to find a text from Maity that simply said:

592

A simmering mix of emotions bubbled up from within me and made its way out in the form of a frustrated grunt. It was a mix of fear, anxiety, confusion, but most of all, anger. As if it was not enough to thrust me in such a dire situation, the man was also sending me cryptic messages whose head or tail I could make nothing of! I let out a grunt again and decided to confront Maity about this when the time was right. I looked up from my phone to find that the Havana hat was nowhere to be seen.

Where had the man gone?

I looked here and there for a few seconds, but there was no sign of either Jayant Sinha or Maity. Another announcement blared through the loudspeakers. The race would start in a few more minutes. Almost involuntarily, I found myself walking towards the no smoking sign. The place was thronging with people now. I avoided collision and made my way to the sign to find the cigarette lying on the ground, a thin swirl of smoke still rising from it. I looked here and there, stumped the burning cigarette out with my shoe and looked at the message again.

592

Nothing! It meant nothing to me! Why did he have to do this?

Suddenly, from the corner of my eye, I saw the Havana hat again. I turned my head to catch just a split-second glimpse of it before it disappeared behind the clubhouse building's wall. I quickly walked towards the wall and stepped into a large hallway with rooms and passages on both sides of it. There was no one in the passage to my right, but the swing door at the far end of the passage to my left was slowly shutting with a gentle but distinct squeak. Had Jayant Sinha walked in through that door? There was no way to tell. I wondered what to do. The 'Members Only' sign on the door made things further difficult for me. I realized I was wasting time. Without thinking any further, I tiptoed to the end of the passage to the left, swung the door open and entered a large room with several chairs neatly arranged around a conference table. The sound of the crowd and of the announcements were all muffled here. There was no sign of anyone in this part of the building, let alone Jayant Sinha. I was wondering if I should turn around and go back when a group of three men came in through one of the doors on the far wall and stood in the middle of the room. They were all clad in the best of casual clubwear—beach shirts, Sunday shorts and straw hats. Two of them had glasses in their hands, the liquid inside those glasses was probably whisky. The third gentleman was much older than the other two and was probably of European origin. Their conversation had stopped because all three of them had seen me.

'Looking for something, are we?' said the older man, in chaste British pronunciation. All three men's eyes were now on me. My stomach seemed empty as I knew I shouldn't be there.

'The gentlemen's room?' I somehow managed to mumble, although my mouth and my throat had both become completely parched.

The old man pointed towards another door and I hurriedly walked towards it. The sound of the three men resuming their conversation reached my ears and I breathed a momentary sigh of relief, only to have my heart stop again. I was now standing in a men's washroom. To my right were the stalls and the urinals. To my left were three large mirrors in ornate frames placed before three meticulously clean wash basins. And right in front of me, placed against the wall, was a beige-coloured suitcase. Old-fashioned Aristocrat suitcase.

Jayant Sinha's suitcase!

'Don't worry, honey! I'll take care of the cake. Like I said, I will.'

A pair of sports shoes was peeping out of the bottom of the first stall. From the way the shoes were moving, I could tell that the person to whom those feet belonged was the one who had said those words. Probably into a phone. Somehow, it seemed to me that neither those shoes nor that voice belonged to Jayant Sinha. This was a younger man's voice. I turned my head sharply to the right. There was no one at the urinals. The only place Jayant Sinha could be then was in the other stall, at the far end of the washroom.

'Well, when have I not, you tell me?' the voice continued. 'No, you are the one who is always speaking of such things. I never do!'

592!

As my eyes suddenly fell on the combination lock of the suitcase, the meaning of Maity's cryptic message suddenly became clear to me. My head suddenly began to reel. Maity wanted me to open the suitcase and look inside!

But, hang on a second! What if it was not what I thought it meant? How could Maity have possibly got the lock combination to Jayant Sinha's suitcase? Impossible! Perhaps those numbers meant something entirely different.

'I'll tell you what, I'll get the cake on my way home this evening, all right? Would that satisfy her majesty?'

What do I do? What do I do? What do I do?

Was there enough time? When had Sinha stepped into that stall? How far along his business was he? There was no way to tell. I would have to make a decision quickly. If I tried to open the suitcase and he stepped out and caught me in the act, I would be done for. Should I go back? Or should I just go ahead and do it?

'Yes, yes, yes! I think you should totally do it!'

My heart felt like it would leap out of my chest and drop to the shining floor of the washroom.

'Don't think so much!' said the voice. 'Do it! Call Preeti and invite her over—and that stupid husband of hers, too!'

I gnashed my teeth and darted forward. On reaching the suitcase, I gently picked it up and carefully placed it on the marble platform beside the washbasin. Then, with swift hands, I turned the dials to 5, 9 and 2, even as the verbal volley of the young man on the phone continued. Then I shut my eyes and pressed the button and the moment it opened with a click, maniacal laughter echoed through the washroom and scared the living daylights out of me.

'Hahahahahaha! Remember what had happened at Colonel Kapoor's party? Oh god! Hahahahaha!'

Now!

With one swift tug, I unzipped the suitcase and flung the lid open, hoping that the sound of the zipper wouldn't be heard over the young man's hearty laughter.

A few shirts, trousers, underwear, toothpaste, toothbrush, shaving cream, safety razor, hairbrush. A pair of slippers. A couple of heavy encyclopaedias. Volumes 1 and 2. The morning's newspaper. A few blank sheets of paper with the name and address of a publishing company on the letterhead. A couple of notebooks and diaries. There was nothing else in the suitcase. What was I looking for? I had no idea. Only one thought travelled through my brain and through my entire body right now—because a familiar sound had reached my ears and turned my limbs numb.

Jayant Sinha had flushed his toilet!

I immediately froze. And realized that my luck had run out—the door to the stall had been flung open, and that I was finally doomed.

The sound of heavy footsteps reached my ears. The man was now standing right behind me. I shut my eyes.

'Excuse me?'

I realized I was sweating profusely. My hand and feet were trembling, and I would black out any moment now.

'Excuse me?' the voice seemed to come from far away. I cursed, cursed, cursed Maity for having put me in this position.

'Could you pass me a few towels, please?'

I looked to my left. The hazy image of a man in a floral shirt and sunglasses began to form in front of my eyes.

'Hang on a second, honey!' the man said again. 'There's a guy in here who's probably had one drink too many! You okay, sir?'

As I slowly regained my strength, I realized what had happened. I gently shut the lid of the suitcase and gave the man a couple of paper towels from the dispenser on the wall. As the young man wiped his hands, he looked at me and then at the suitcase. There was no sound from Jayant Sinha's stall. Which could mean only one thing. He was listening!

'Do you want me to . . .' the man gestured towards the suitcase and began.

'No, thank you,' I quickly cut the man off before he could say anything further. 'I'm fine.'

'Are you sure?'

'Yes!' I insisted. 'I'm much better now, thank you. I can help myself out.'

The man gave me a look that doubted the claim. But then he slowly shook his head and said, 'All right! You take it easy now! It's only afternoon!'

Having said this much, the young man crumpled his towels into a ball, threw them in the wastebin and walked out of the room. And as soon as he did, there was pin-drop silence in the room. How on earth was I to zip the suitcase now? Sinha would step out any second now!

As soon as the sound of flushing reached my ears again, I placed my left hand under the hand dryer and the mechanical sound of the stream of air filled the room. I yanked the zip with my other hand, closed the suitcase, clipped the lock and turned the numbers on the dial randomly. The moment I placed it back where it was earlier, the dryer stopped and Jayant Sinha came and stood next to me.

I didn't spend a single second more in that washroom. Without looking at Sinha or the suitcase, I quickly rushed out of the door into the conference room, then past the swing door, down the passage, into the hall and out into the open veranda, where I grabbed a wall and finally caught my breath.

Phew! That was a close shave! Had Jayant Sinha seen me fidget with his suitcase? Probably not. The deeper I breathed, the more I began to calm down. I smiled and then laughed at myself. Had it not been for the unknown young man in the washroom speaking to his wife or girlfriend or whoever, I would have been in big trouble. But a second thought made me stop laughing and turn serious again. Why had Maity asked me to open Jayant Sinha's suitcase? What did he expect me to find inside? I myself hadn't noticed anything suspicious.

I looked at my phone. The race was almost about to begin, but there was no further message from Maity. I realized I had had a bit of a shock, and that I would have to sit down somewhere and catch my breath. It had been an exhausting day, and I wasn't quite sure what Maity wanted me to do next. I decided to sit in the stands where Maity had asked me to and wait for him to get in touch with me.

I entered through the gates leading to the course itself, where the horses would be galloping to the finish. The gates were all numbered. I walked through the crowd and made my way to Section 14. These were the lower stands, closest to the track. I turned my head to look up at the upper levels of the gallery. Some of the box seats seemed quite comfortable and expensive. Most of them were empty, though. Maity never said or did anything without a reason, so I assumed there must be a good one for his asking me to sit in that specific place too. I climbed down a couple of steps, found my way to the fifth row, dusted the bench with my handkerchief and took a seat. I looked at the far right of my row. There was an innocent-looking, schoolmaster-type, elderly gentleman sitting there all by himself with an umbrella and a race book in his hand. He was lost in the book, peering at its pages and muttering something to himself. I looked left: most of the people in the crowd seemed like regulars here. The rows below had people strewn here and there too, and there were more people coming in as the clock was ticking closer and closer to 2 p.m. Even the announcements were becoming louder, so much so that the loudspeakers were beginning to screech.

As the faint sound of neighing reached my ears, I now saw the horses towards the far left. Only their heads were visible behind the swivel doors that would all flick open when the race began. The horses themselves were of various colours—most of them were brown or black. They looked beautiful with their flowing manes. The helmets of some of the jockeys were visible too.

'Whips have been banned. Same with spurs. Half the charm is gone!'

I was about to turn around on hearing a gruff voice when a strong hand landed roughly on my neck and stopped me from doing so. I grimaced in pain and let out a little cry.

'It'll take me two seconds to snap your neck,' the voice said. 'And I won't even have to use both my hands. No one will hear you, no one will know. So sit still and watch the race.'

A siren blared from somewhere over the crowd. Everyone suddenly seemed to turn towards the course itself. Some people began to yell out swears and cusses. Yet others began to whistle and cheer. In all the mayhem, a few other words came floating to my ears, even as I broke into a cold sweat.

'Huckleberry!'

'Gold Rush!'

'Sikandar!'

'Andromeda!'

I realized they were the names of the horses. My horse's name was also called and cheered for. The stands were now almost full, although most of the people were standing. A gentle breeze had just blown in from the west and sent a shiver down my spine. I realized my neck would probably be very, very sore in the morning.

'I see you've bet on Jewel Thief,' the voice spoke into my ear. 'So have I. Good tip. From that busybody pal of yours, I'm sure!'

My legs seemed like they were melting. My breathing had become heavy. With a final blare of the horn, the doors flicked open, and with a huge uproar rising into the skies over the Maidan, nine horses shot out from behind the doors and galloped away. The crowd roared and cheered, threw earthen cups, hats, caps and handkerchiefs into the air. From the left corner of my eyes, I could see something dangling right behind my ears. I realized it was the strap of a pair of binoculars, through which the man was now watching the race. I could feel his warm breath on my neck now. I shifted my glance to the other corner of my eyes, far towards the right. The schoolmaster gentleman was sitting at the far end of the bench. He was looking straight at me!

'Help!' I mouthed, silently.

The gentleman must have seen the look of fear in my eyes, even if he could not decipher my silent plea for help. But his eyes now turned to the man behind me, and I don't know what he saw, but he swallowed hard, picked up his umbrella, stepped off the gallery and walked away into the cheering crowd. A sudden piercing pain rose at the tip of my spine and almost rendered me breathless. I realized that I simply wouldn't be able to scream, and even if I somehow managed to, no one would be able to hear me. I panicked, but couldn't do a thing about it, as my hands and feet seemed to have turned numb. There were hundreds, perhaps thousands of people all around me. Would I have to die like this? In so gruesome a manner?

'Atlas!' I heard the gruff voice again. 'That's the name of the bone on your spine that's hurting now! That's what happens to those who try to poke their nose in other people's business!'

As I choked, and the afternoon sunlight seemed to die down right in front of my eyes, I saw the race finish and heard the entire gallery erupt in a massive roar of cheers.

'Congratulations!' The voice seemed to come from far away. 'We've both won!'

I could feel my neck creak. The sound a twig makes just before snapping into two. I realized I had barely a second or two more. If that.

'Imagine having read about the atlas in an encyclopaedia!' A second grave and familiar voice reached my ears, and I am not quite sure what happened inside my head after that. The grip on my neck loosened just a little bit, and from somewhere, I don't know from where, I suddenly got the strength to make one last-ditch effort to survive. I summoned every little ounce of strength from various parts of my body, gathered them all into my right fist, clenched it hard and swung it around to land a blind blow on the face of the man sitting behind me.

I felt the binoculars drop on to the bench next to me. The grip immediately loosened further, I freed myself, staggered away, tripped on something and fell back on the grass. A few people helped me up, asking me if I was okay. I didn't—or rather couldn't—respond to any of their questions. Instead, I gasped for breath and looked around to find the man who had tried to kill me in the middle of the racecourse crowd. Maity's wicked, wicked penchant for dark humour and wordplay, no matter how mistimed, had probably saved my life. As my blurry vision cleared a bit, and the people who had helped me up dusted my shirt and my jeans, I saw a man sitting on a bench rubbing his jaw, and Maity quietly sitting behind him, watching him. As the sun was directly behind the man's head, I couldn't see his face properly.

'You all right, Prakash?'

A cool and calm sense of relief descended on me like a cascade from a waterfall, as I heard my dear friend's voice.

'Yes, Maity!' I said, still struggling to breathe. 'Thanks for the help!'

'I didn't do a thing!' said Maity. 'Didn't even lay a finger on this man. Whatever you did, you did it all by yourself!'

The man now rose to his feet and turned towards Maity, still adjusting his lower jaw from that powerful punch of mine.

'Not that I couldn't have, though!' said Maity, his voice now serious and growling, his eyes locked directly with the man's in a menacing glance. 'Your game is up, Jayant Sinha! Look over your shoulder and you'll realize how fundamentally flawed and formulaic our Hindi films can be. Yes, those are cops! Armed cops! And no, they don't arrive on the scene late. Sometimes they arrive on the scene well before the villain does!'

[13]

Jayant Sinha had now been brought to Park Street Police Station. He was now being held in the interrogation room. Maity and I were waiting for Satish Mukherjee to come and meet us. Maity had called the Inspector and briefed him about everything that had happened at the racecourse; he was on his way. I was sitting on a chair with my head hung and my face buried in my palms. Maity was sitting next to me, nursing my neck with a cold wet towel.

'It's not without reason they named it atlas,' he said. 'Just like that Greek god is said to carry the planet on his shoulders, that particular vertebra of the spine carries the entire weight of the skull. Not an easy job if you ask me. You are lucky he aimed for that spot! Of course, if he had tried to do something more dangerous, I would have stepped in much—'

I waived his hand away and said angrily, 'You knew he would be there, didn't you?'

'Yes!' Maity seemed amused by my disappointment. He placed the towel and the bowl of water aside. 'Remember the thing that was sticking out of his suitcase in the photographs? I got a chance to take a closer look at it the other night. It was a race book! Man's a compulsive gambler!'

'And yet you sent me there?' I asked, making no effort to mask the hurt in my voice.

Maity remained silent for some time. Then he said, 'I had no other choice, my friend. I wanted him to make a mistake. And I knew that he had realized that I was after him—that's the reason he left the hotel in a hurry. So, I couldn't take a chance confronting him myself. He would have simply tried to escape or, worse still, clammed up. No, that was just not good enough. I wanted to catch him red-handed.'

'But why?' I asked. 'What possible hand could he have had in Mrs Sullivan's murder? He was in his room, fast asleep, when Edith Sullivan was being murdered. We saw that, didn't we?'

'Aha!' Maity smiled and said: 'Don't forget what Diane Arbus said! A photograph is a lie about a lie! Ask yourself, what did you really see? Did you *see* Jayant Sinha fast asleep when Mrs Sullivan was being murdered?'

'No, but Sayantan said—'

'Sayantan said he went to bed by ten every night!' said Maity. 'Doesn't mean he was asleep at the time of the murder. There's a difference.'

I thought about it for a second and realized how right Maity had been all this while. I said, 'And Sayantan is dead, so there's no way to confirm it from him either.'

'Do you see now what I am trying to say?' Maity said.

'So, what are we going to do now?' I asked.

'We are going to talk to Sinha and find out what he knows about the murder of Edith Sullivan.'

'You think he somehow had a hand in Edith Sullivan's murder?' I asked.

'It is . . .' Maity frowned and hesitated, 'it is just a little theory of mine. The time for that has not yet come. But it will soon. He may have had a hand in the murder, he may not have had. But one thing is true.'

'And what is that?' I asked.

'He ran!' Maity said, nodding his head. 'Why did he run?'

'And moreover,' I asked, 'how did he come to know that we were looking for him?'

Maity seemed to shake his thoughts off and turned towards me, 'Well, we will cross that bridge when we get there.'

'But I don't understand something,' I persisted. 'How on earth did you know the combination to the lock on Jayant Sinha's suitcase?'

Maity smiled and said: 'The human mind is a very strange thing, Prakash. And human beings have the most astonishing habits. Did you know that nine out of ten people will open their combination locks, and completely forget about scrambling the combination once they have opened their locks? I understand why they do this peculiar thing. So that they don't have to bother about rearranging the combination again when they want to secure the lock. Just to save a few seconds.'

'Oh my god!' I said, 'You are right! Why, I do this too— all the time!'

'Nine out of ten people would do that!' said Maity. 'But it is this peculiar habit that can become a big problem. At any given point of time, if you see a suitcase in an unlocked position, then there is a 90 per cent probability that the number on the dial is the combination to the suitcase. All that you have to do is to see the suitcase in an unlocked position.'

'Like you did in the photographs of Jayant Sinha's room?'
I surmised.

'Exactly!'

I shook my head and said, 'Good lord! I'd never given
any thought to it.'

Maity changed the topic and said, 'Anyway! How did
your day go?'

'Other than the fact that my neck almost got snapped
into two?' I said, 'Not too bad.'

'Did you find the couple?'

'Eventually, I did,' I said. 'Took some doing, but I did
find them.'

'And?'

Over the next half hour or so, I gave Maity a detailed
description of everything that had happened since I had
walked out of Sayantan's apartment, till the time Maity and
I met at the racecourse. I did not leave out anything, even
the slightest detail, because I knew that Maity had sent me
on that job wanting me to be his eyes and ears. And that
Janardan Maity's eyes and ears were the sharpest I had ever
come across. Maity listened to the entire thing with rapt
attention, asking a question here or seeking some more detail
there—minor things. Or at least, things that seemed minor to
me. To him, perhaps the solution to the entire puzzle lay in
those little details. In the end, he patted me on my back and
said, 'I'm really proud of you, Prakash. Even I could not have
handled the entire thing better.'

After waiting for a few more minutes, we heard a car
stop outside the station's entrance. Satish Mukherjee walked
in and the men in the room outside struck him smart salutes.
We were waiting in his office, and as he entered, he walked

straight up to me and put his hand on my shoulder gently. 'I heard what happened. Are you okay?'

I nodded and thanked him for his concern. He sat in his chair, gulped down the glass of water on his table and said, 'I have good news! Robert Sullivan has been arrested!'

'What!' Maity and I jumped out of our chairs. 'Excellent, excellent! From where?' Maity asked.

'We didn't find his name on the passenger manifests of any of the flights or trains that left the city over the last few days. So we figured there was a possibility he was hiding somewhere in the city itself. Just like you had told me he could be.'

I looked at Maity with a questioning glance. Maity nodded at me and said, 'It's nothing, Prakash, it was just a hunch of mine. Where did you find him?'

The last question was directed at Satish. He said, 'In a small hotel near Dum Dum.'

'And that Jhunjhunwala gentleman?' Maity asked.

'Still absconding,' said Satish, as he lit a cigarette and leaned back in his chair.

'Absconding?' I asked.

Satish nodded, 'Harish Jhunjhunwala is wanted by the Kharagpur police in relation to the smuggling and distribution of heroin. Mostly to students. He is a dealer. He has been dealing in it for several years now. Recently, one of his friends was caught selling drugs outside the IIT campus. Since then, Jhunjhunwala has not been seen in Kharagpur. The police are looking for him. It now seems he was hiding in Kolkata, at the Fairy Glen.'

'Any connections or affiliations with either Robert or Edith Sullivan?' Maity asked.

'Not that we know of,' Satish flicked his fingers to drop some ash into the tray before him. 'Nor with Jayant Sinha. We are investigating further, of course. I have even issued a red alert. He won't be able to leave the city. We will find him.'

I asked, 'Did you find something useful from T. Subramaniam? The writer?'

'Not much!' said Satish. 'We have gone through all his stuff. He is writing a novel all right, my men checked his manuscript. He seemed shocked to learn about the death of your photographer friend, said he had met him just yesterday. Didn't know any of the other guests. Knew the Sullivans and Sinha only by face. A "hi" or a "hello there". That's all.'

'Where is he now?' I asked.

'We had to let him go, I'm afraid. Didn't have enough to keep him in. I have asked him not to leave the city, though. He said there was no question of his checking out of the hotel till he had finished his novel.'

'Good, good!' Maity said. 'But when can we speak to Robert Sullivan?'

'He is being brought to this station as we speak. Meanwhile, let's not waste time. I am going to speak to Jayant Sinha. I'm assuming the two of you would like to come along?'

'What say, Prakash?' asked Maity. 'You want to take another swing at him?'

'Oh, for heaven's sake, Maity!' I said in an irritated voice, even as Satish and he seemed to share a good laugh, that too at my expense!

'Come, come now, my friend!' said Maity. 'Don't be angry. These are not the movies. I could have helped you, but isn't it better that you helped yourself?'

'That's not even my point,' I said, as we followed Satish towards the interrogation room. 'You used me as bait!'

'That I did, my friend,' Maity's voice suddenly changed. 'That I did!'

The thick steel door to the interrogation room had been thrown open with a heavy clang. A constable struck a smart salute; Satish returned it and stepped in. Maity was still standing at the doorway, hesitating to go in. I was wondering what had gotten into him—even Satish had turned around, and was waiting for Maity to step in, and although it took him a couple of seconds to do so, Maity did step in. But not before saying a few more words that seemed quite mysterious to me.

'I hope you will forgive me for doing so!'

□□□

Ever since I had known Maity, I had seen the interiors of several police stations. I had even had the opportunity to be in several interrogation rooms. The interrogation room of Park Street Police Station was clearly one of the better-looking ones. I knew these rooms were deliberately kept unclean and bare to create an unsettling atmosphere for those who were being interrogated. But this particular room was nothing of that sort. It was fairly large, had a water cooler in one corner, a couple of steel almirahs and cabinets in another, even air conditioning. In fact, the room looked more menacing from the outside than the inside. As the door clanged shut behind us, Maity was looking around the room, whereas my eyes were fixed on the man who had tried to kill me in cold blood earlier today.

Jayant Sinha was sitting on one of the two chairs on one side of a large table. On the other side, there were two more chairs. Satish Mukherjee went and sat on one of them. He flicked his phone open and started scrolling through it. Sinha was looking straight at Maity, who did not even seem to be looking at him. He was still busy looking around the room. A uniformed inspector was standing near the door and watching us silently. A uniformed constable went over to one corner of the room where a video camera had been placed on a tripod. He pressed a button and a red LED lit up on the camera.

'What's behind that door over there, Satish?' Maity asked, pointing to the wall to our right.

'Which one?' Satish looked up from his phone for a second. 'Oh, that's the toilet.'

Maity nodded. Satish had gone back to scrolling through his phone again. I heard him mutter under his breath, 'During the interrogation, criminals tend to want to use that!'

Sinha had heard him too. He was fuming all this while. Now he said, 'May I ask why I have been brought here?'

'Of course, you may!' Satish responded, without taking his eyes off his phone's screen. From the way the light on his face was changing, I could guess that he was swiping through his photo album.

'Well?' said Jayant Sinha, in a frustration-laden voice. 'Why have I been brought here? What did I do?'

'You didn't do anything,' said Satish, calmly. 'Because we stopped you from doing it!'

'Really?' said Sinha. 'And what did you stop me from doing?'

'You tried to kill me,' I said, in as grave a voice as I could summon. 'Earlier today, at the races. Tried to snap my neck.'

'What?' Sinha smiled. 'It's true I had been to the races. In fact, my horse won! But I didn't try to kill this man! I don't even know this man!'

'There are people who saw you attack him, Mr Sinha,' Satish said calmly.

'Eight to ten chairs will fit in here, no?' Maity asked. The question was directed at Satish again.

'Yeah, yeah,' Satish said, and even I was wondering what was going on. I could only imagine what must have been going through Jayant Sinha's head. He suddenly no longer seemed menacing to me any more.

'You mean this man?' Sinha pointed towards Maity. 'He saw me? Of course, he'll say anything and everything in favour of this young fellow here.'

'Why?' Maity's voice echoed through the room, as he walked around the walls, reached the table and took the chair next to Satish's.

'What do you mean, why?' asked Jayant Sinha.

'You said I would speak in his favour,' Maity said, pointing towards me. 'But you also said that you don't know him. What makes you think, then, that I will support him?'

Jayant Sinha was at a loss for words for a few seconds, and Maity took the opportunity to corner him even further. He said, 'Oh, and by the way, it wasn't just me who saw you try to kill Prakash. There were others, too. Two of them are in this very room.'

Maity pointed towards the constable standing in the corner with his back to the wall. I hadn't noticed him properly so far. I now looked at the man and was shocked to find that he was the same innocent-looking schoolmaster with the umbrella! My eyes then turned towards the door, where the Inspector was standing! He waved at me with a smile—a smile that I had seen before. In the washroom at the racecourse! This was the same man who was speaking on the phone—the one with the sports shoes and the floral shirt! I now realized Maity had planned the entire thing carefully, well in advance, and he had personally gone after Sinha because he wanted to be in control of the entire operation.

'Ok, Mr Maity,' Jayant Sinha finally said. 'I agree I know you. And Mr Ray too. Let's cut out the bullshit and speak man to man, shall we?'

I looked at Satish. The phone was still in his hands but his eyes were now on Sinha. Maity leaned back in his chair and said, 'An excellent suggestion! Let's do that!'

Jayant Sinha said, 'May I ask you what you were doing in my room at the Fairy Glen when I was out?'

It was now my turn to be surprised. What on earth was the man talking about? Satish glanced at Maity too, but didn't react.

Maity was calmness personified. He said: 'You were the *first* person I suspected. A man who functions like clockwork! Now *that* is a man I am interested in. My friend Prakash knows me very well, he knows how much of a stickler I am for punctuality. It's a rapidly disappearing virtue in this day and age, and who knows, might soon go extinct! I cannot even begin to tell you how much I appreciate the fact that you, Mr Sinha, are a punctual individual. A man of discipline.'

'Yeah, so?' said Sinha. 'That gives you the right to break into my room?'

'No, no,' Maity lifted his forefinger and corrected the man. 'Not right! But the opportunity! I knew *exactly* when you would be in your room. And *exactly* when you wouldn't. And during one such opportune period of time, as you correctly pointed out, I picked the lock of your room and 'broke in', as you so aptly described.'

'But why?'

'Because I wanted to look inside your suitcase,' said Maity. 'I knew the combination to the lock on your suitcase, so it was obviously easy for me to open it and take a look at the contents.'

'But I don't understand,' said Sinha. 'How did you know the combination to my lock?'

A soft smiled appeared on Maity's face. He stared at Jayant Sinha for some time and then said, 'Let's not worry about that for now, Mr Sinha. But to answer your earlier question, yes, I did break into your room and I did look in your suitcase. And you came to know that I had come into your room, and so you followed me, outside your hotel on Park Lane. But what you did not know, Mr Sinha, is that I too saw you follow me. It was then that I realized that my little expedition to your room had been discovered. But alas, before I could reach you, you checked out of the hotel. You left in such a hurry that you even left some of your things behind. So now, it is time for me to ask you some questions. First things first, what can you tell us about Edith Sullivan's murder?'

Jayant Sinha had been frowning all the while. Now his frown grew deeper as he said, 'Who?'

'Edith Sullivan,' Maity said. 'The wife of Robert Sullivan.'

'She's been murdered, you say?'

'Mr Sinha,' Maity said patiently, 'you *know* she has been murdered. By her husband. You were right next door! And the walls of the Fairy Glen are unfortunately so thin that there is no way you could not have heard all that yelling and screaming and quarrelling from the Sullivans' room! No matter how deep your sleep is. And I don't think it is that deep either. People who function like clockwork don't enjoy deep sleep. So, let's not try to make things difficult here, shall we?'

Jayant Sinha tried to put up a defiant face to Maity and Satish: 'I know nothing of any murder. I don't know any Sullivan or anyone else. I come to the city once every month for my job. And I don't bother anyone, nor do I want anyone else to bother me.'

'Mr Sinha,' Maity said again, 'you know what I see you doing right now? Like, right this instant? I see you digging a hole. And I can assure you that you will fall into it. We know Robert Sullivan murdered his wife! Are you trying to tell me that a woman was punched on her face by her husband after a noisy quarrel and then later that night, he came back into the room and killed her in a fit of rage, and you were *so* fast asleep that you did not hear any of this? None of it? You expect me to believe that?'

'All right, all right,' said Sinha, as he stammered, 'I . . . I don't want to get into any trouble. Yes, I heard them quarrelling. They were yelling at the top of their voices. The woman, in particular, was swearing and cussing at her husband. Civilized people don't use that kind of language. And if I were to be perfectly honest with you, I felt bad for the old chap. I mean the tongue on that woman! You should have heard some of the things she was saying! But I also swear to you, in the name of God, that I know nothing about any murder. I heard the fellow punch his wife. I heard the door slam shut, and I heard the wife weeping. Suits her fine, I thought! I smiled and went back to sleep. And I woke up straight in the morning, when my alarm rang. That's god's honest truth.'

Maity frowned and said, 'Please continue.'

'A few days later, I came back from work one day and found that my room had been broken into.'

'How did you know this?' asked Maity. 'I would like to believe that I am an extremely careful man!'

'You may be careful,' said Jayant Sinha, 'but I am smarter! When I lock my suitcase every day before leaving for work, I turn the combination to a specific number. It's the wrong number, but I have a habit of sticking to the same number. That day, I came to my room and proceeded to unlock my suitcase, only to find that the number had changed. I immediately knew that someone had meddled with it.'

'Interesting!' Maity smiled. 'Very interesting! How did you know it was me?'

'I spoke to the receptionist,' said Sinha. 'He knows me, I'm a regular. I didn't ask him straight out; he would've gotten disturbed. But he's an old man, he loves to talk. So bit by bit, I coaxed the information out of him, over a drink no less. He said a few people had come looking for trouble, causing all sorts of ruckus. He said they claimed to be undercover policemen, but he did not think that they were. He said he had spent his entire life managing reception desks at hotels, so he knew what cops looked like! He even described you and Mr Ray and another friend of yours. The moment I heard all this, I went to my room, packed my bags and left. I live in Chandannagar. Once I reached home, I realized I had left my shirt and my sandals behind in the room. So the next morning, I came to collect them and as soon as I entered Park Lane, I saw that the entire place was crawling with cops. Then I heard someone had been murdered right next door to the hotel. I realized I was in trouble, because I had left in a hurry, so I panicked.'

Jayant Sinha now turned towards me and said, 'I don't know if you will believe me, Mr Ray, but I only wanted to scare you, so that you and Mr Maity don't bother me any more. I knew you had opened my suitcase. I knew it the moment I saw my dial. I just wanted to threaten you, shake you up—so to speak. My intention was not to kill you.'

I looked at Jayant Sinha's face. He did seem as if he was telling the truth. Maity and Satish, too, looked at each other. Then Maity turned towards Sinha and said: 'What can you tell us about the murder of the man who lived in the building next door?'

'Absolutely nothing!' Jayant Sinha replied. 'I only heard about it on the street from some bystander.'

Satish asked, 'Where were you from midnight to 4 a.m. this morning?'

'At home,' said Sinha. 'In bed.'

'As we have found out on at least one occasion before,' said Maity, 'just because you are in bed doesn't mean you are asleep. Is there someone who can corroborate the fact that you were indeed at home when the murder in the next building was committed?'

'You mean do I have an alibi?' asked Jayant Sinha. 'Unfortunately, I don't. I am not a family man and my landlady does a bit of weed after dusk.'

Maity tapped on the table a few times and said, 'Did you know the young man who was murdered was a professional photographer?'

'No, I didn't,' came the response.

'Hmm. I have one final question for you.'

'And what is that?'

'Mr Sinha,' Maity leaned forward in his chair and stared directly into Jayant Sinha's eye. 'Since how long have you been going to the racecourse?'

Jayant Sinha was probably expecting a much more threatening question because he seemed a bit relieved, even a tad surprised, on hearing Maity's question. He said, 'Oh! Well, let's see now. It's been almost twenty years. But I'm not an addict. I don't think anyone can say that I am one. As I told you, I come to the city only once every month.'

Maity smiled and said, 'You don't need to be physically present at the racecourse to bet on horses, Mr Sinha! But then how can someone as smart as you expect someone like me to know that, no?'

Maity was clearly done. Satish asked the constable to take Jayant Sinha out. As the constable switched off the camera, Satish said, 'You will remain in custody till this investigation is over, Mr Sinha.'

'But, but,' Jayant Sinha protested, 'I haven't done anything.'

Maity said, 'As I always say, Mr Sinha, if you haven't done anything bad, then you have nothing to worry about. That's a promise!'

[14]

'Well?' asked Satish Mukherjee, when Jayant Sinha had been removed from the room. 'What do you think?'

'That man knows a lot,' Maity stood up and stretched his back. 'He isn't telling us everything.'

'Oh, you don't need to worry about that,' said Satish. 'We know how to make him talk.'

'Or dance,' the Inspector quipped from near the door, as Satish and he both scoffed.

I looked at Maity, who seemed lost in his thoughts. From the way he was pinching his lips and cracking his knuckles, I knew he was preoccupied with some new idea—perhaps a new line of thought.

'My methods,' said Maity calmly, 'are a little less medieval.'

'But Mr Maity,' Satish said, 'I must admit to you that absolutely nothing is making sense to me right now. It's all very complex and confusing, and it's making me very uncomfortable.'

'I feel the same way too, Maity,' I said. 'It's all so foggy. And by the way, when did you break into Jayant Sinha's room?'

Maity looked at me and said, 'The first evening, after we had been to the hotel for the first time; I dropped you off at home and came back to Park Lane.'

'But why?' Satish asked. 'And why Sinha's room specifically?'

Maity looked at Satish and said, 'I was looking for something!'

Both Satish and I asked, almost in unison, 'What were you looking for?'

'I can't talk about that right now,' Maity said.

'Good god, Maity!' I exclaimed. 'You and your theatricality! Why do you have to do this every single time? Why this suspense?'

'I don't do it for fun is what I can tell you both,' said Maity, gravely. 'Sometimes, the less people know, the better.'

Satish looked at Maity and Maity stared back at him. I knew my friend well enough to expect such whimsical behaviour from him. And I had become used to it as well. But clearly, Satish had not. And he was having a hard time adjusting to it. I also knew very well that it was Satish who would have to adapt to Maity's ways because it simply wouldn't happen the other way around.

'One thing we have to admit,' Satish said finally, 'that thing he did with the combination lock was actually quite intelligent. Jayant Sinha doesn't come across as an intelligent man, does he?'

Maity remained silent for a few seconds and then said, 'No, he doesn't. Appearances . . . they can often be quite deceptive!'

An officer stepped in and reported to Satish that Robert Sullivan had been brought in. Satish asked the officer to bring Sullivan into the interrogation room right away, and then turned towards Maity.

'How do you want to handle this?' he asked.

'Would you mind if I lead?' Maity said.

'Not at all,' responded Satish, and we prepared to meet Robert Sullivan for the first time.

Robert Sullivan had been taken to the room, and the moment I laid eyes on him, I realized that nothing could have prepared us for such a sight. He looked older, bigger and broader than he did in the photographs. Much, much bigger! To be honest, he looked like a medium-sized monster. His head almost touched the ceiling of the room. And it took two of Satish's strongest and most muscular men to restrain him. The man did not show any signs of struggle, though. But he did make me shudder. It seemed to me that if he did choose to struggle, then he could knock out every single person in this room with his bare hands in less than half a minute.

'Mr Sullivan?' Maity asked, 'Mr Robert Sullivan?'

'Yeah?' Robert Sullivan's voice matched his physical appearance. It sounded like a heavy conch had been blown somewhere.

'My name is Janardan Maity. This is Senior Inspector Satish Mukherjee. He is the officer in charge of this police station. And over there is my dear friend Prakash Ray, who's a writer. Would you have a seat, please? We have a few questions for you.'

Robert Sullivan looked at our faces in turn and said something strange, 'I thought they'd put handcuffs on me!'

We looked at each other, and then Maity was the one to speak: 'The police don't use handcuffs unless they deem their use an absolute necessity, Mr Sullivan. You seem to be cooperating with us, at least so far. And I think I can speak for my colleagues here and assure you that we do not see the possibility of that changing any time soon. So why don't we all take our seats around this table here, comfortably, and . . . you know . . . talk?'

There was a heavy silence in the room for some time. The two men who were grabbing Sullivan's arms (with both their hands, no less) looked at Satish, who gestured at them. They slowly let go of him.

'Please,' Maity showed him a chair and smiled.

The two men and two other constables walked back to the door, shut it from inside and stayed in the room. A third constable walked to the video camera and switched it on.

'Now,' said Maity, 'as I said, I have a few questions for you, Mr Sullivan. Would you please answer them for me?'

'Why not?' The conch blew again.

Between the questions and the answers, there was pin-drop silence in the room. It was hard to believe that just outside this room on the street, there was a constant stream of rush-hour traffic, honking, etc. Inside, it was almost deathly silent.

'Are you married, Mr Sullivan?' Maity broke the silence with his first question.

'Yes,' said the man. 'Twenty-four years now.'

'And what is your wife's name, if I may ask?'

'Edith Margaret Sullivan,' came the answer in clear and punctuated enunciations.

'Do you know the current whereabouts of your wife, Mr Sullivan?'

Silence. Deathly silence. Silence for the longest time.

'I'm not quite sure I understand.' I didn't know that Robert Sullivan's voice could become any heavier. Turned out, it could. 'What do you mean when you say that?'

Maity smiled patiently and asked again, 'Do you . . . know?'

'Of course, I do! Why wouldn't I? What kinda husband would I be if I didn't know where my wife was?'

Maity nodded and said, 'Indeed, that is quite true. Could you tell us where Mrs Sullivan is right now?'

'She's with her sister, in Bangalore. That's where she is. She's from there, originally. I'm from Mumbai. We had plans to go to Bangalore first, spend a couple of weeks at her sister's and then head to Mumbai to meet my old uncle Jimmy. He's a baker. James Sullivan. He's sixty-three!'

Satish now leant forward in his chair, extended his phone towards the man and said, 'Mr Sullivan, could you please confirm if this is your wife's sister's address in Bangalore?'

As the large man leant forward to take a look, the chair under him creaked as if it would break under his weight. I saw one of the officers remove his right hand from behind his back and place it softly on his holster. The butt of a sidearm was peeping from inside the dark brown leather holster.

'That's the one,' said Robert Sullivan. 'Only it's spelt F-R-A-S-E-R, and not F-R-A-Z-E-R.'

Once again, silence. With an almost invisible gesture of his eyes, Satish gave a brief signal to his officer, who removed his hand from his holster and stood at ease again.

'Look, Mr Sullivan,' Satish now turned his attention to the enormous giant of a man sitting in front of him. 'I don't want you to be alarmed. But we have checked with your wife's sister in Bangalore, who lives in Fraser Town. Mrs Sullivan is not with her sister. She never got there. What is of greater significance and interest to me is that nor did your sister-in-law seem to be aware of any plans of the two of you going to Bangalore, or to meet her, or stay at her place. We know that the two of you were staying at Hotel Fairy

Glen, on Park Lane. We have also been informed by some of the other guests staying in the hotel that there seemed to be some sort of domestic quarrel between the two of you. And then the next morning, you and your wife checked out at an odd hour. And she was not in the pink of health, according to the receptionist, to whom you—interestingly enough—said that you were headed for the airport to catch a flight to Bangalore! But none of the passenger manifests have your names. And then, more than a week later, you were found staying in a hotel near the airport, when clearly you have a home in Howrah.'

The man muttered something.

'Excuse me?' said Satish.

'Hotel Monarch!' Robert Sullivan said, staring directly at Satish.

That blasted silence again. I could hear my heart beating inside my chest. The tension inside the room was palpable.

'Indeed!' said Maity. 'Hotel Monarch! That's where you were found staying. We spoke to your neighbour, the nurse. She said there have been quarrels between the two of you in the past too. And that these quarrels were quite . . . shall we say . . . frequent. Sometimes, they would even become . . . violent!'

Robert Sullivan hung his head. Then he said, 'Edith had dreams!'

I looked at Maity. His eyes were glued to the man's face, as if he was trying to read his soul.

'She wanted things,' the big man continued. 'Fame, money, glamour, nice gowns, perfumes. She wanted to be a model or a singer or an actress. She could have been, I suppose. Had she not met me. I . . . I don't understand things too well,

you know? I am . . . slow. But she liked me because I don't
touch the drink. Never have. Saw it take Daddy. I did what
Edith told me to. She's the clever one. Some things, the good
Lord decides for you. Some things, you decide for yourselves.
What's good for you, what's bad. Edith knows. She's clever.
No one can knock the wind out of her.'

Maity looked at me, his face grave. Satish and the rest of
the men were silent spectators by choice. It was obvious that
they wanted Maity to run the show.

'Mr Sullivan,' Maity spoke in a gentle voice, 'your wife
never got to Bangalore. Where is she?'

'Like I told you,' the man said, 'she's at her sister's.
In Bangalore.'

Satish stood up and started pacing up and down the
room. It was quite obvious that he was at the end of his
patience. Maity paused for a second and then said, 'Do you
know a man named Sayantan Kundu?'

'Who?' frowned Robert Sullivan.

'Sayantan Kundu,' Maity repeated. 'He was a professional
photographer. He passed away this morning. In his apartment.
Right next door to the hotel you and your wife were staying in.'

There was a brief silence, after which Robert Sullivan
asked, 'Was he sick?'

Satish and Maity were watching the man's facial
expressions closely. I personally couldn't see any deceit in the
man's expressions. Truth be told, when I looked at him up
close, he seemed like a child. Big in size, perhaps. But the
mind of a child. Somehow, it seemed to me that Maity also
thought the same. He shook his head and said in a gentle
voice, 'No, Mr Sullivan. He wasn't sick.'

Robert Sullivan looked around the room and said, 'This room is big. I'm not used to big rooms like this one here.'

Maity continued to stare at Robert Sullivan's face for a few more seconds. Then all of a sudden, he said, 'Very well, Mr Sullivan, you are free to go!'

Satish had clearly not expected this. The other cops in the room too seemed perplexed at this unexpected announcement. Satish took Maity aside and they whispered something to each other. I stepped forward to join their conversation.

'Well, goodbye then!' Robert Sullivan said.

'No!' Satish growled, as he pointed towards Robert Sullivan. 'You stay right where you are!'

Then he turned towards Maity and exclaimed, 'What on earth do you think you are doing, Mr Maity? I can't let the prime suspect in a murder investigation walk out of my station just like that!'

'Satish,' said Maity calmly, 'you have to trust me on this; you are not going to get to the bottom of this by using conventional methods.'

'But why?' Satish Mukherjee looked like he couldn't believe what he was hearing. 'We have the photographs! We have the murderer sitting twelve feet away from us! What else do we need? I have a case here, Mr Maity. And I'm sorry but I will not let you ruin it just because you have a whim.'

Maity hung his head. Then he said, 'Even if I assure you that tomorrow you will lose?'

'What do you mean I'll lose?'

'The law!' Maity said. 'It is a strange thing, my friend. You, of all people, ought to know that. The law demands evidence. Not just circumstantial evidence. Hard, tangible evidence—one that proves the suspect guilty or innocent without a shadow of doubt. And I can assure you, you don't have enough evidence to convict this man. So, you take a call, because it's your decision. Do you want this man to walk out of the courtroom free of all charges? Or do you want him to walk out of this room tonight, so that we can perhaps hope to get to the bottom of this case?'

Satish looked frustrated. From the corner of my eye, I could see Robert Sullivan watching us debate over his fate. Even the officers and constables looked distinctly uncomfortable and were whispering to each other.

'What do you want me to do?' Satish finally asked Maity.

'Careful what you wish for!' said Maity. 'If you want me to tell you what *I* want you to do, then you have to follow my advice word for word. So, think carefully before you commit—can you do that?'

'Have I never done that before?' came the response. I could sense the angst and hurt in Satish's voice. I know how much respect he had for Maity and his judgement. But even I felt that what Maity was doing right now was sheer madness!

'You have,' Maity stepped forward and placed a soft hand on Satish's shoulder, 'but I want you to do it again. Without asking any questions. I want you to place your complete trust in me. And I assure you, all will be well in the end.'

'Very well,' said Satish quietly. 'Tell me what you want me to do.'

Maity took a few seconds to choose his next words carefully. 'I have two requests of you. First, let Robert Sullivan go. For tonight.'

'Shall I ask one of my men to keep an eye on him?'

'There is no need for that. Just gently ask him to come back here to the police station tomorrow one last time. To sign some papers, to complete some formalities, whatever—make something up.'

'But why?'

'That's what I was coming to. Tomorrow, at exactly 4 p.m., I want you to arrange a meeting here.'

'A meeting?' Satish asked. A familiar thumping had started inside my chest. Satish might not know what this meant, but I did.

'A meeting, yes!' said Maity. 'I want the following people present in this meeting: Malcolm Brennan, Robert Sullivan, Jayant Sinha, Harish Jhunjhunwala, Kishore and Riya Rajbanshi, and, last but not the least, our writer friend Mr T. Subramaniam! Of course, you and I and Prakash will be there too.'

'How on earth am I supposed to find Harish Jhunjhunwala overnight?' Satish seemed exasperated at Maity's whimsical demands. 'Man's been missing since the last three months.'

'Correction!' interrupted Maity. 'The police couldn't find him since the last three months. He was staying at the Fairy Glen less than a week ago. You are the police, it's your job to find him. Do your job.'

'All right, all right!' Satish replied willy-nilly and proceeded to execute Maity's orders.

Maity pulled me aside and said, 'Poor chap looks pretty upset!'

'Well, now he knows what I have to put up with!' I said testily.

'Oh, come on!' said Maity. 'You enjoy these little whims of mine, don't you?'

'Maity?' I said. 'You've solved it, haven't you?'

The camera was still recording everything that was happening in the room. Maity stared at it for a long time, his eyes narrowed, a soft smile gently floating on his lips. To me, this look of his was very familiar. It meant the calm before the storm. When he responded to my question, it seemed like his voice was coming out from the other side of a screen of fog.

'Not yet, my friend! But I'm close. So close that I can feel it! I can feel the tingling in my fingertips. I can feel the rush of blood! But we need to be careful, we need to be on our toes, because the job's not done yet. There's still one last thing that remains to be done. One last piece of the puzzle that has yet to be found! And not only found, it has to be placed in the right spot, too. It has to fit, so to speak!'

'And then?'

Maity's eyes glistened as he still watched the camera. 'And then, we will be able to see the whole picture!'

[15]

That evening, after stepping out of Park Street Police Station, Maity started walking towards the west, so I started walking alongside, without disturbing his train of thought. I had a suspicion as to where he was headed, and when he reached the Rafi Ahmed Kidwai Road crossing and took a right turn, my suspicion proved correct. On reaching Park Lane, Maity turned right again and I entered the lane with him.

'Do you have a driver's licence, Prakash?' he asked, as we walked towards the Fairy Glen.

During my early journalism days, I had joined a driving class and gotten a driver's licence issued in my name. I told Maity this and he remarked, 'I'm thinking of buying a car. Nothing fancy, a small one would do for the two of us. Sometimes I'll drive, sometimes you drive it. Since we have to run around so much, this dependence on taxis is something we could avoid.'

A good idea, I thought. Nowadays, one didn't need to have a huge income to be able to afford a car. Dozens of banks would happily give you a loan to buy a car. Janardan Maity was strictly against any kind of loans, though. As he himself said quite often, he was an old-fashioned man, with old-fashioned values. And one of them was to cut your coat according to your cloth. The man didn't even have a credit card!

I knew Maity had enough money to buy a car without having to take a loan. His ancestors were affluent zamindars, and I knew that Maity would never lack for money. Nor was he what might be called a wasteful individual. The only two things that I had seen him spend a lot on were books and food. 'You know something, Prakash?' he often used to say, 'most of the good things in life don't cost much!' This was the first time I heard him talk about a car. The advantages were plenty and Maity was right—we were having to depend a bit too much on cabs.

Dusk had fallen and instead of thinning, the evening crowd in Park Lane seemed to have swollen. As I saw Sayantan Kundu's building, my heart sank. The young man may have been foolish, he may have even chosen the wrong path at the crossroads of life, but he didn't deserve an end like that. I knew Maity had also been quite shaken by Sayantan's death, although he would never show that on the outside.

'Aren't we going in?' I asked Maity. He had crossed the entrance to the hotel and walked ahead.

'No,' replied Maity, as he stood in front of the narrow lane between the two buildings. I went and stood beside him. Maity watched the lane for some time and then stepped into it. It was decidedly filthy, so I had to watch where I was stepping. Maity seemed unbothered though. He walked straight ahead, looking around. Around five or six yards into the lane, he stopped and looked back. I followed his gaze and realized he was looking at the main road itself. Then he started looking around again. I decided to stay where I was, because I knew that even if I joined Maity and asked him what exactly he was looking for, I wouldn't receive a response.

'This lane,' Maity said from a distance, 'it's not as narrow as it seems at first glance.'

'So?' I asked and immediately realized my mistake. As expected, Maity didn't respond. Instead, he looked up at the two buildings on both sides of the lane and stared at them for quite some time. Finally, he walked back towards me, glanced at his watch and said, 'Let's go, Prakash. If we hurry, we may still make it to the library.'

Why Maity wanted to go to the library, there was no way to know. I did know that he wouldn't answer, even if I asked him. Fortunately, even during rush hour, we managed to get a cab and reached the National Library well before closing time. Maity asked me to hang around in the reading room and said he needed to borrow a few books. I spent a few minutes browsing through a couple of magazines and then sat down in one of the chairs, feeling exhausted.

What a day it had been! Starting with a brutal murder, to running around the city looking for Kishore and Riya Rajbanshi, to almost getting killed myself at the racecourse, and then the two bizarre interviews, and finally, here I was sitting in the library flipping through the pages of a magazine without actually reading anything. I realized my body was just not being able to take it any more. Thankfully, Maity returned soon enough, with three books in his hands and said, 'Let's go!'

I glanced at the books from the corner of my eye. Two of them were on photography, the other was simply titled *Optics*. I realized that while I was planning to go home and go straight to bed after dinner, Janardan Maity would probably read through the night!

The next morning, I woke up quite late to find that I had as many as three missed calls from Maity. I was immediately worried, so I quickly called him back to ask him if everything was okay.

'Mahadev seems to be cooking some mysterious mouth-watering dish!' he said. 'I can smell it from my bed! Why don't you come over? We can have lunch together and then head out to Park Street.'

'You called me thrice to tell me this?' I asked, exasperated.

'Mouth-watering, Prakash!' he said. 'You have to smell it to believe it! If you haven't had your breakfast yet, I prohibit you from having anything. Save your appetite.'

The man's quirks knew no bounds. I told him I would come over in an hour or so. Then I sat in bed for some time, my head feeling heavy. Maity seemed to be in a good mood, although I knew that there was a distinct possibility that he hadn't slept all night. He had told me he was waiting for the last piece of the puzzle. I figured he had finally found it!

But I was wrong! It was a few minutes past noon when I walked into Maity's home in Bhowanipore. He himself answered the door and welcomed me in with a smile. He did seem to be in a good mood, but when I asked him whether he had found the solution to the case or not, he simply said, 'Almost!'

'Give me something to think about too,' I said. 'I am completely in the dark.'

'Why don't we do it the other way around?' he suggested.

'What do you mean?'

'Why don't *you* tell me what you think about this case?'

I thought for a few seconds and said: 'Well, to put it in a nutshell, a professional blackmailer named Sayantan Kundu saw a woman named Edith Sullivan being murdered by her husband Robert Sullivan, in a fit of rage.'

'Seemingly,' Maity added. 'Seemingly in a fit of rage.'

'Very well,' I nodded. 'Seemingly in a fit of rage. But Robert Sullivan claims that he hasn't murdered his wife. But at the same time, we also know that he has no idea where his wife is right now.'

'Again,' Maity shut his eyes and corrected me patiently, 'that's not quite true. He *seems* to know where his wife is, but we know for a fact that his wife isn't there.'

'Right! And I don't know what you felt, but the man seemed a bit . . .'

'Slow,' said Maity, his eyes still shut. 'That's the precise word that he used to describe himself. *Slow!*'

'Then, of course, there's Jayant Sinha. He said he attacked me because he panicked, but I don't buy that. He's a strong man, though, I'll tell you that.'

'It is usually the physically strong ones that are also the mentally weak ones,' Maity said. 'But never mind, carry on!'

'He admitted to hearing the couple fight,' I said, 'but he claimed that he knows nothing about the murder.'

'Either of them,' Maity added.

'Right!'

Maity reached inside his pocket, pulled out a hundred-rupee note and extended it towards me. 'He also didn't get a chance to cash out his winnings yesterday!'

'Is that what I won?' I said, surprised.

'You bet you did!' he smiled. 'Fair's fair! Your ticket had fallen on the ground, I picked it up and collected the amount. Don't get addicted though!'

'I'm never going back there ever again!' I said, taking the note from Maity.

'I thought so!' Maity laughed out loud. 'I also think you are on the right track when it comes to solving this mystery. There are quite a few significant things you said there, a moment ago. However, the one thing that is constantly throwing you off the rails is the fact that everything you saw—*you*, mind you, not Sayantan Kundu—was in still images. Moments frozen in time.'

I thought for a few seconds and said, 'Do you think Sayantan might have seen something that he didn't quite understand the significance of?'

'That's an excellent point, my friend,' Maity rose from his couch and started pacing up and down the room. 'That is what my hunch is too. And hunches are an integral part of solving a puzzle; we should not look down on them or ignore them. But the more important question here is: Did the true meaning of something that Sayantan saw occur to him at a later point of time?'

'What do you mean?' I asked.

'What I mean is this: Is it possible that Sayantan Kundu saw something through his camera but didn't quite understand the significance of it at the time he saw it, but much later, perhaps many days later, the realization dawned on him?'

I sat up and said, 'And that's why he was murdered?'

'Could it be?' Maity said.

'But what was it that he saw?' I asked.

Maity smiled sadly and said, 'If only we knew that, my friend! If only we knew that!'

'Is that the last piece of the puzzle you were referring to?' I asked.

Maity did not respond, he simply continued to pace around the room. After some time, I said, 'Can I tell you something, Maity? Somehow, and I don't have a solid reason to say this, but somehow, it simply doesn't seem to me that Robert Sullivan could have murdered his wife! The man's way too simple to have done something like that.'

Maity stopped next to his window and looked out. His eyes wore a sad look. For the longest period of time, he simply kept staring out of that window. Then he said a few words in a low, whispering voice, almost as if he was speaking to himself, 'When does simple become *too* simple?'

Before I could ask him what he meant, Mahadev entered the room and announced that lunch had been served. Maity rubbed his palms together, flashed a smile and said, 'Come Prakash, let us go and do some justice, finally! We have a long day ahead of us!'

My heart had started thumping again. I knew I had not been able to theorize virtually anything about the case in our discussion. All I had were isolated data points. Haphazard, independent, with no relation to each other. But Maity was clearly able to see a picture in this chaos. Like an image that slowly emerges on a photo paper inside a dark room. In the beginning, we see only parts of the image, separate from each other. And we cannot identify them. But slowly yet surely, the image in its totality begins to form, right in front of our eyes. And we can then see it, and recognize it for what it is. I knew Maity was several steps ahead of me in that recognition process, and that this evening, he would uncover the whole image for us!

The dish that good old Mahadev had cooked for us was an authentic Bengali preparation of the koi fish, straight from Dhaka. The koi fish was known to have extremely strong bones, so I had to focus on the food.

Maity too seemed to forget about the case for the time being and relished the food, talking instead of a couple of car brands that some of his friends had recommended to him. I listened to him but absent-mindedly. In my heart, various images flashed for a fraction of a second and disappeared in an instant. Bob Sullivan's face as he was smothering his wife to death. The hazy image of racehorses galloping by as the daylight was dwindling in my eyes. Sayantan Kundu's bloodied body lying crumpled in his filthy bed. Mrs Chatterjee's charming smile. Mr Subramaniam's menacing look out of the glass façade of Café Columbus. Kishore and Riya Rajbanshi's ecstatic expressions as they made love to each other. Nalin Shukla's grin. Malcolm Brennan peering at me over his thick eyeglasses. A local train shooting past Kishore's poor parents as they looked on. The undercover police constable in the schoolmaster's dress smirking at me. And finally, Edith Sullivan's helpless look, complete with a black eye, tears rolling down her pale cheeks, a cross hanging from a slender chain around her slender neck.

I did enjoy the dish. But I couldn't get these images out of my head—no matter how hard I tried. I shut my eyes a couple of times. Really hard. To try and erase those disturbing images. But I couldn't. I picked up the glass from the table and took a few sips of water. And as I did, I found Janardan Maity watching me silently.

'Eat, my friend,' he said, in a soft, gentle and familiar voice. 'Everything will be fine! Everything is fine!'

[16]

We were all gathered in the interrogation room of Park Street Police Station. Chairs had been brought in and arranged in a semicircle around the large table. Someone had removed the camera from the corner of the room. There was one key addition to the room since yesterday, and I learnt that Maity had specifically requested Satish for it—a large whiteboard. Maity stood in front of the table staring at his wristwatch. Seated around and facing him were Kishore Rajbanshi, Riya Rajbanshi, Jayant Sinha, Robert Sullivan, T. Subramaniam and Malcolm Brennan. There were a few empty chairs in the room. Satish and I went and occupied two of them. I learnt from Satish that despite his best efforts, Harish Jhunjhunwala was still absconding and that he had duly informed Maity about it.

At exactly 4 p.m., Maity started speaking.

'Good evening! Thank you, everyone, for coming at such short notice. And a special note of thanks to Senior Inspector Satish Mukherjee for allowing us to convene here this evening. As you all may have guessed by now, you all have—at some point of time in the last few weeks—stayed at the Hotel Fairy Glen. The manager of the hotel, Mr Malcolm Brennan, is also present with us—you all know him. Also present are Mr Robert Sullivan, an agent for the Life Insurance

Corporation of India; Mr T. Subramaniam, an aspiring novelist; Mr and Mrs Rajbanshi, who have appeared in a few relatively unknown motion pictures; and Mr Jayant Sinha, an encyclopaedia salesman. We are gathered here to solve the mystery behind not one but *two* murders. The story that will end here in this room this evening actually began several days ago, when a young man named Sayantan Kundu had come to me and my dear friend Prakash Ray, and admitted to having committed a serious crime. Sayantan was a professional photographer, and as I learnt later on seeing some of his photographs, he was quite good at it too. However, he was having trouble getting by on his photography alone, which—as many of you may know—can be an expensive vocation with minimal returns, especially if you are among those who still haven't given up the good old habit of shooting on film. Sayantan Kundu was one of those photographers, and, by his own admission, he was starving.

'Around a year or so ago—and this is what Sayantan told Prakash and me—there was a cyclone, during which the coloured pane on the only window in Sayantan's room had shattered to pieces. It was then that he discovered that from his room, he had a perfect view of six rooms of a hotel across the alley below. That hotel was the Fairy Glen.'

A few soft murmurs were heard in the room. Kishore and Riya looked at each other and whispered something. Someone cursed under his breath.

'It was then that a devious plan began to take shape in Sayantan's mind,' Maity continued. 'It is my belief that the kind of things that he could see going on in those six rooms was exactly what put this idea in his brain. An idea that finally spelt his doom. You see, hotels are strange places. You stay there, but don't live there. You are constantly passing through. A hotel room takes you on a journey, so to speak—only that it's a private journey. Once you have locked the doors of your hotel room, you feel a sense of power and freedom. A freedom that you somehow do not feel when you are at your own home. At home, you are accountable and responsible for your actions. There are certain restrictions to what you can and cannot do. But not in a hotel room. The moment you enter a hotel room, there is a certain excitement that does not necessarily come from seeing just the clean sheets and a new bed that you can sleep on. No, it's something different, something more powerful. All of us have felt this at some point in time in our lives. And it is this strange mix of emotions that also sparks a certain carefree attitude in guests. Which is why, sometimes, crimes tend to happen in hotel rooms. And some of these crimes are violent ones.

'But it's not merely crimes that take place in such rooms. Your domestic life—the life that you normally lead— also spills over to these rooms. It's not that you become a changed person, no. Your quarrels, your griefs, your joys, your achievements, your failures, your love life—everything spills over to these rooms, sometimes magnified because of the new-found freedom I was talking about a moment ago. Sayantan Kundu began to witness some of these images of the human condition from his small peephole. He became what can be best described as a voyeur. But he did not stop at that. He was an excellent photographer. So he started photographing people in certain acts that they would not want others to know about.'

'That's just outrageous!' cried out Kishore Rajbanshi, and his wife joined him too. 'It's a direct violation of people's privacy!'

'Son of a bitch!' Jayant Sinha grunted.

Malcom Brennan took off his glasses and shook his head wearily.

T. Subramaniam smiled as he watched the other guests, until Kishore noticed him and barked at him: 'What the hell are you laughing at? Is there something amusing? You find this funny?'

'Sorry!' Subramaniam quickly said. 'I was just . . . I'm sorry!'

Maity raised his hand and said, 'Calm down, please. And let's move on, we have much to talk about this evening. You see, Sayantan started blackmailing people, threatening them to release their photographs to their loved ones, or to the police, or all over the Internet. By his own admission, he would always choose his victims carefully. He would, for instance, never try to blackmail a group of people who were doing a drug deal, because then there would be a threat to his life. Nor would he ever try to extort money from those who would not be able to pay him. No—his victims were mostly unfaithful, adulterous men, sometimes women. Those were the people whom he was successfully able to fleece.'

'Good lord!' said Malcolm Brennan. 'Disgusting!'

'But on the nineteenth of June, Sayantan Kundu saw something horrible through his camera, and he shot a few photographs of a crime taking place, a crime that truly rattled him. He came to me with those photographs. Perhaps he was afraid, afraid that he had been found out. Perhaps he wanted justice to prevail—he wanted the murderer to be caught and punished. Or perhaps his conscience, or whatever was left of it, had suddenly told him that what he was doing was wrong. Whatever be the case, Prakash and I saw those photographs. In those photographs, we saw Robert Sullivan murder his wife, Edith.'

A few gasps and murmurs were once again heard around the room. Everyone looked at Robert Sullivan as Maity pointed towards him. Malcolm Brennan looked the most disturbed.

'I didn't murder my wife,' Robert Sullivan said in a heavy yet calm, childlike voice. 'Like I told you, she is at her sister's place, in Bangalore.'

Maity stared at him for some time and then continued his speech. 'The night of the nineteenth is the night when all of you were staying in one or the other of the six rooms that were visible from Sayantan Kundu's window across the alley. That night, Robert and Edith had a quarrel—like the many quarrels that they were used to having, as confirmed by their neighbour. Edith said something to Robert that enraged him. And he punched her in the face.'

'I can vouch for that,' said Jayant Sinha, pointing to Robert Sullivan. 'I heard him punch his wife.'

Riya Rajbanshi too slowly raised her hand and said, 'I . . . I'm not sure, but I think I heard it too. There was some sort of . . . disturbance . . .'

Kishore immediately whispered something to Riya sternly, and the lady quickly lowered her hand.

Maity continued, 'After assaulting his wife, Robert left the room, and Edith tended to her wound and cried herself to sleep. But later that night, Robert came back to the room, and in what seemed like a fit of rage, took a pillow and smothered his wife to death! He then seemed to realize what he had done and panicked for a few moments. He also realized that he would have to get rid of his wife's corpse. So he dressed her up in an overcoat, covered her head with his own hat, her face with a scarf, and then simply walked past the reception with his arm around his wife's dead body, telling Mr Brennan on the way that his wife wasn't feeling too well and that they had an early morning flight to catch.'

'My god!' said Brennan, clutching the armrest of his chair. 'But I could've sworn . . . oh Lord!'

The rest of the people in the room seemed at a complete loss for words. Everyone frowned and looked at Robert Sullivan. Jayant Sinha rose from his seat, pointed at Robert Sullivan and said, 'I refuse to sit next to this man!'

'You are free to sit anywhere you want, Mr Sinha,' said Maity. 'But you will leave this room only when I have finished saying what I have to say.'

Jayant Sinha took another chair next to Kishore Rajbanshi and wiped his forehead. Maity went on.

'When Sayantan Kundu brought me these photographs, Prakash and I decided to investigate. Our job was to find Robert Sullivan and bring him to justice. But there was something else I had seen in the photographs that had piqued my interest and made me curious.'

'Mr Maity?' Satish Mukherjee intervened and said, 'May I have a word with you?'

Everyone in the room, including myself, was wondering what was going on. Maity seemed the least amused, because clearly, Satish had broken his flow of words and disturbed his train of thought. I had seen a constable enter the room and whisper something in Satish's ear, but I thought he would know better than to disturb Maity.

'What is it?' Maity frowned and asked.

Satish quickly went up to him and whispered something in his ear. Maity's frown deepened, and he nodded slowly. Satish signalled the constable waiting for his orders and the latter went to the door, opened it and in stepped someone who almost had me fall off my chair.

'Bob?'

I could barely hear the voice over the heavy thumping inside my chest.

'I told you!' said Robert Sullivan. 'I didn't murder my wife!'

There was pin-drop silence in the room. I looked at Satish, his jaw had dropped! I looked at Maity, his face looked ghastly pale too. I myself could not believe my eyes. The lady who had walked in was none other than Edith Sullivan!

'What are you doing here, Bob?' said Edith Sullivan. I recalled her husband had said she wanted to be a singer. Her voice was as sweet as that of a lark!

'They asked me to come here, Edith,' said Bob Sullivan, rising from his chair and walking over to his wife, who placed a soft palm on his cheek. 'They are not being nice to me!'

Edith Sullivan slowly turned towards us now, looking at us in turns. Her eyes seemed like they were breathing fire! When the next words came out of her mouth, the sweetness in her voice was all gone.

'What is going on over here?' she demanded. 'What are you doing to my husband? He's not some kind of freak, you know?'

'Ma'am,' said Satish, 'are you Mrs Sullivan? Mrs Edith Sullivan?'

'He's a gentle soul,' she cried out, as she held her husband's hand firmly in her own. 'Gentler than any I've ever seen! And yes, I am Edith Sullivan! Are you the man in charge here?'

'No, Mrs Sullivan!' Maity's voice was heard from across the room. 'I am the man in charge here. Whatever you have to say, you can say it to me.'

Jayant Sinha scoffed and said, 'You don't look in charge any more, Mr Maity!'

Edith Sullivan whispered something to her husband, and then strutted across the room to come and stand directly in front of Maity. Then she looked straight at him and said, 'What is your name?'

Maity answered the lady's question calmly, 'My name is Janardan Maity, madam.'

'Can you explain to me why you have been bothering my husband, Mr Maity?' Edith Sullivan's face was firm and her teeth clenched.

Maity's response was brief, measured and to the point. 'We have reason to believe that your husband tried to murder you in Room 203 of Hotel Fairy Glen, madam. On the night of the nineteenth of June. I can still see the sign of a physical assault under your eye. What I, however, do not understand is why on earth would you be denying this? Is it to protect your husband? Or is it because you are scared? Of someone? Or something?'

Edith Sullivan's steely glance faltered for a second. Then she said, 'Are you a family man, Mr Maity? Are you married?'

'No, madam, I am not.'

'Then I'm afraid you know nothing about the relationship between a husband and his wife.' A note of contempt crept into Edith Sullivan's voice. 'One falls, the other helps him up.

One breaks down, the other collects the broken pieces and mends them—one by one, piece by piece, with love, with care. Of course, I don't expect *you* to know! Bob and I have had our share of ups and downs. Like any other couple. I don't know how you know this, but it's true, that night, he did hit me. But what you may not know, and what this poor old man will never tell you, is that I hit him too. And do you know why he wouldn't tell you? Because he loves his wife. And he knows that his wife loves him too. We all have our shame and our sorrows, Mr Maity. We all are walking through the darkness in search of light. You, me, every single person in this room, in this world. So pray tell me, who do you think *you* are to pry into our private lives?'

In front of a room full of people, Maity hung his head. Edith Sullivan's eyes were still spewing fire. Satish quickly walked up to her and said, 'But Mrs Sullivan, your husband said you were at your sister's place in Bangalore, and we called her—'

'Bob forgets things,' Mrs Sullivan said. 'We missed our flight and stayed in a hotel that day. Fares had increased and we couldn't afford another flight. In any case, my sister did not know that we were coming, so we decided to cancel the Bangalore plan. As Bob and I had had a quarrel the previous night, I told him I wanted to go visit my friend; she lives in Salt Lake. Bob apologized for hitting me, like he always does, but I still insisted on going alone. So I left, assuming he would have gone back home to Howrah. But last night, I got a call from him saying that he had been brought to the police station. So I came back to the hotel looking for him. When I didn't find him there, I came here.'

'Hotel Monarch!' said Robert Sullivan, gently.

Satish looked at Maity, defeated. Edith Sullivan gave Maity one last spiteful look and said 'Are we free to go now? Or do you still want to continue harassing my husband?'

Maity hung his head again. Satish watched him and let out a deep sigh. He signalled to the constable, who opened the door to the room. Edith Sullivan walked back to her husband, held his arm and walked with him towards the door. The rest of the people looked around in confusion. Kishore Rajbanshi said, 'I . . . I don't understand! What about us? Are we free to go too?'

'Of course we are free to go!' said Jayant Sinha and quickly walked towards the door.

'I told you, Mr Maity,' said Malcolm Brennan, as he stood up. 'But you didn't believe me! I saw the two of them walk out! Together! Why didn't you believe me? What a waste of everyone's time!'

Only T. Subramaniam didn't say anything, and kept looking at Maity with a grave, serious look on his face.

'You can go too,' Satish told him, and he rose from his chair to leave.

I felt absolutely shattered and empty. Maity had never been in such an awkward situation before. Perhaps he had made some errors in his calculations, that could happen—he was only human. It hurt to see him being insulted and made a fool of in this manner. I walked up to Maity and said, 'What's going on, Maity? What is all this?'

As Maity looked up, I was forced to take a step back. Because I saw fire, sheer fire burning in his eyes, as he said the next few words to me, 'The final piece of the puzzle, my friend!'

And then, in that interrogation room in the heart of Park Street, I heard Maity's roar. In a voice that was so, so familiar to me, in a voice that brought back so many memories of all the adventures we have had together in all these years. A roar that I hadn't heard in a long, long time. A roar that sent shivers down the spine of the most hardened criminals, the most vicious murderers, the vilest of minds. And it instantly filled me with a sense of purpose once again.

'Not so fast, ladies and gentlemen! No one will leave this room until I say so. Mrs Sullivan, perhaps you did not hear me say this clearly enough the first time, so I'm going to say it again . . .'

Everyone turned around and looked at Maity, as the next few words came out of his mouth and literally shook the room.

'*I* am in charge here!'

[17]

Maity's voice was so powerful, his authority so decisive and final that the constable immediately shut the door behind Robert and Edith Sullivan's backs, just as they were about to turn and walk out of the interrogation room. Everyone stared at Maity, including every member of Satish's force.

'Please,' Maity said, with the same authority but in a gentler voice, 'return to your seats. I have not finished speaking yet. Mrs Sullivan, you may please sit next to your husband here. As for the others, please sit where you were sitting earlier.'

It may seem incredible, but not one person in the room—not even Satish Mukherjee—uttered a single word or protested in any manner whatsoever. Everyone came back and took their seats. I went back to my seat next to Satish. Maity stared at the people in the room for some time and then proceeded.

'As we now know, Mrs Edith Sullivan is alive and well. But right at the beginning of my speech, I had told you that we were gathered here to solve the mystery of *two* murders. And I cannot let you leave until we have solved the mystery of the *second* one—the murder of Sayantan Kundu. The photographer turned blackmailer, who first brought the photographs of the events of nineteenth June to me.

Who told me that from his room, he had seen Edith Sullivan being murdered by her husband. I can only wish he were here to realize that what you see can be an illusion too. But alas, that is not to be. Because yesterday, he was found dead in his apartment, his throat slit, right through the windpipe. So here's my one big question. If Edith Sullivan is still alive, and therefore Robert Sullivan never committed any murder, then *who* murdered Sayantan Kundu? And more importantly—*why?*'

There was deathly silence in the room. Everyone was watching Maity, and Maity in turn was watching everyone's faces one by one.

'Now, you see, I have a hunch about this. And like I was telling my friend Prakash earlier this afternoon, hunches are an integral part of the puzzle-solving process. One mustn't ignore them. Hunches, conjectures, hypotheses—these are important. When someone says, I have a bad feeling about this, then that actually means something. There is usually a reason behind one feeling that way. Or perhaps several reasons. Our brain may not be able to perceive or comprehend these reasons in a tangible form but that does not necessarily mean those reasons do not exist. Even as Sayantan Kundu was sitting in my drawing room and telling me his bizarre story, I had a hunch. A hunch that kept itching away at the back of my head. A hunch that didn't let me sleep at night. A hunch that kept me awake and on the hunt over the last few days.

'But before I tell you about my hunch, or let's call it my hypothesis, I think it would benefit all of us gathered here if we could *see* for ourselves what Sayantan Kundu saw through his peephole. Unfortunately, he is not here to tell us in his own words, so the next best approximation that we can aim for is if I drew a diagram of the six rooms he could see through his camera, as seen on the night of nineteenth June, when he *thought* he had seen Robert Sullivan murder his wife. Please bear with me, my drawing skills are far from good.'

Having said this much, Maity proceeded to pick up a marker from next to the whiteboard and reproduced the diagram that he had drawn up for me the other day.

301 Harish Jhunjhunwala Check-in: 9 Jun Check-out: 21 Jun	302 Vacant	303 Kishore & Riya Rajbanshi Check-in: 19 Jun Check-out: 20 Jun
201 T. Subramaniam Check-in: 25 Feb Check-out: Staying	202 Jayant Sinha Check-in: 16 Jun Check-out: 27 Jun	203 Robert & Edith Sullivan Check-in: 18 Jun Check-out: 20 Jun

Maity finished the diagram, popped the cap back on to the marker and turned around to face us again. I noticed that he had added two details in the diagram since I had last seen it—the check-in date for T. Subramaniam and the check-out date for Jayant Sinha.

'That's the best I could do,' he said. 'But I think it'll do, for the sake of this investigation. Now, as you can see, Mr T. Subramaniam has been staying in Room 201 for a long time, he is a writer—writing a novel. In Room 202, we have Mr Jayant Sinha, who sells encyclopaedias. He lives in

Chandannagar but comes to the city once every month, and stays exactly a week. Comes on the sixteenth of every month, and leaves on the twenty-third. For some reason, which we will get to in a few minutes, he overstayed this month. He is a man of impeccable discipline and punctuality. Does everything on time. And not just on time, dot on time.'

'Why do you keep saying that?' Jayant Sinha asked. 'Is that a crime? To be punctual?'

'On the contrary!' said Maity. 'It's a virtue! A rapidly disappearing virtue, as I was telling you yesterday. But as I said, we will come to you in a few minutes. In other words, when the time is right! Let's move on to Room 203, the scene of the alleged crime, which we now know never happened! Robert and Edith Sullivan were staying in this room. They had checked in on the eighteenth and checked out—in quite a dramatic fashion—on the twentieth.

'On the top floor, a man named Harish Jhunjhunwala was staying in Room 301, which is a suite. The police have information about this man—he is a drug dealer from Kharagpur. And he was, in fact, hiding in that room. He used to spend most of his time watching movies on the television set in his room. He is the only one among the guests who is not part of this congregation this evening. The next room was vacant—but an interesting fact has come to light, thanks to my dear friend Prakash. A guest named Mrs Daisy Zorabian had checked into that room. But merely a few hours later, she complained of disturbances from the room next door and checked out. She was perhaps referring to the noises coming from the room next to hers on the same floor—the honeymoon suite!'

Kishore and Riya Rajbanshi looked embarrassed and flushed. Maity went on, unfazed.

'Mr Kishore Rajbanshi and Mrs Riya Rajbanshi had gotten married that very day—the nineteenth of June—and checked into the honeymoon suite of the Fairy Glen. In a conversation with Prakash, the couple have admitted to hearing the quarrel between the Sullivans, thanks to which, Mrs Rajbanshi insisted on checking out early, on the morning of the twentieth. That's it! That's the list of guests.'

Maity paused to catch his breath. I turned around to see that even the constable was listening to every word Maity was saying with rapt attention. Everyone else in the room had their eyes fixed on Maity.

'Now,' Maity resumed his speech, 'I have a few questions to ask each of you. And for your own sake, I hope you will avoid embarrassing yourself and give me honest, truthful answers. Remember, you are sitting in a police station. And although you may not be under oath, it is a crime in itself to mislead a police officer, especially in the investigation of a crime as serious as murder.'

Satish nodded and Maity continued.

'Mrs Rajbanshi! Let me start with you. Are you familiar with a man named simply as Bruno? That's the name he goes by, although his real name is Gopal Sharma.'

Riya Rajbanshi seemed to shudder a bit. Then she said briefly, 'Bruno is my agent.'

'Correct! Your screen agent. Also, your manager, if I am not mistaken. I spoke to him last night. He told me the titles of the three films that you and your husband have done together. And I looked up those films on the Internet.'

Kishore and Riya Rajbanshi were visibly uncomfortable, especially in the face of Maity's stare. 'There's no judgement here, Mrs Rajbanshi! Who am I to judge? I am merely interested in the facts. Because it is the facts that have direct bearing on this case. The three films that you and your husband have acted in are all pornographic films, aren't they?'

The silence of the couple said it all. Mrs Rajbanshi suddenly said, 'We have nothing to do with any of this.'

'I am coming to that,' said Maity. 'Mr Sinha! Let's talk about you now. You say you have been going to the racecourse for how many years now?'

'Almost twenty years! Why?'

Maity had started pacing up and down the room. He said, 'The other day, you tried to attack my friend Prakash. In the ensuing brawl, Prakash dropped his betting ticket. Not only did I collect it, I cashed it too. But you had not dropped your ticket, although you did not get a chance to cash it, because by the time the race ended, you were under arrest!'

'Two thousand rupees I won that day!' Sinha growled angrily.

'Well, it's your own doing, Mr Sinha!' said Maity. 'But you know what's more interesting to me? That there was something else that you did drop that day. Something that I picked up, and something that you—strangely enough—seem to have forgotten all about!'

A dark cloud seemed to descend over Jayant Sinha's face, as he saw Maity hold something up for everyone to see. It was black in colour, looked small but heavy, and had a strap attached to it. I had seen only a glimpse of it before, although partially.

Maity said, 'It was this pair of binoculars.'

Jayant Sinha looked both nervous and angry now. It seemed like he didn't know what to do or say. Maity continued:

'I tried looking through these binoculars at the horses yesterday, and I could immediately feel the discomfort. No matter how much I adjusted them, that discomfort remained. So, I borrowed some books from the library and read up on the subject of lenses. You see, there are two types of binoculars in use. The first, that give you high magnification. Even something really far away would be seen many times larger in size, and hence rendered clear. And the second, which give you a wide field of view. Such binoculars offer low to mid-level magnification, but the image you can see is wider, as if you are watching a movie. In horse races, it is the second type of binoculars that regular betters usually prefer, because they want to see how one horse is performing *against* the others. This particular pair of binoculars, however, is of the first type, not the second. In other words, these are not ideal binoculars for watching a horse race.'

Jayant Sinha clenched his fist and seemed like he would jump up and attack Maity any second.

'However,' Maity continued without paying any attention to Sinha, 'these are by no means bad binoculars. On the contrary, they are quite expensive. So expensive, in fact, that an encyclopaedia salesman cannot afford them!'

Maity now stopped pacing and looked directly at Jayant Sinha, 'Would it then be fair to say that someone gave you these binoculars? That too quite recently? So recently, in fact, that you had just started using them, only to find that they were not of much use at the racecourse?'

Jayant Sinha didn't respond, only gave Maity a spiteful look. Maity was far from done though. He bent down and brought his face uncomfortably close to Sinha's and said, 'Yesterday, you had told me that you were smarter than me. Today, I want you to know that you are not smart at all, Mr Sinha. You are a moron! Do you really think that I am so careless that you will catch me breaking into your room? No, Mr Sinha! Janardan Maity does not operate like that. I made you think that you had discovered my intrusion into your room. I knew your habit of arranging the numbers on that dial of your suitcase when you locked it. It gave me the perfect opportunity to introduce a little chaos in your plan. You are not as smart as you think you are, Mr Sinha!'

Sinha's breathing had become heavier, but Maity was still looking directly at him with a steely glance. 'And I will see to it that you get what you deserve for laying a hand on my friend!'

'Maity,' I said softly from across the room. He had heard me, and he knew exactly why I had called out his name. And he responded to my unsaid, unpronounced request by keeping his fury in check. He came away from Sinha and took a moment to control himself. Then he turned to face the room again.

'Mr Subramaniam,' he said.

'Yes, sir?' said the writer.

'I went to the library last evening,' Maity said.

'An admirable habit!' smiled Mr Subramaniam. 'Which library?'

Maity smiled back and said: 'You know very well which library, Mr Subramaniam. The National Library, where I have friends, where I have been going for almost three decades now. That library. The one from which you borrowed that book of yours. The one I have seen you read in every single photograph of yours that Sayantan Kundu had taken. And the one you were reading in Café Columbus the other day, when the three of us met you. David Baldacci's *Divine Justice*. How many pages are there in that book, Mr Subramaniam? Around 300, I believe? You've been reading that book since February? Are you a slow reader?'

'Not only am I a slow reader,' said Subramaniam calmly, 'it's a good book.'

Maity nodded, 'I see! But you may want to return that book to the library because it's long overdue. You will have to cough up quite a substantial fine, though. Nothing much, for a man like you. Now that I know who your father is.'

The smile slowly disappeared from T. Subramaniam's lips on hearing those words. And his face became grave.

Maity didn't dwell on him any further and turned to Robert Sullivan instead.

'Mr Sullivan! My final question is for you. I have been to the room that you and your beloved wife were staying in. Room 203. I stood there, in that room, and looked out of the window. And although I *knew* that there was a tiny window on the wall on the other side of the alley, it took me almost a minute to find it. In broad daylight.'

'What are you trying to say?' the man said. Somehow, all of a sudden, it seemed to me that his voice had changed. There was now a hint of fear in it.

'What I am trying to say, Mr Sullivan, is that on the night of nineteenth June, after you were seen by Sayantan Kundu in what he thought was the murder of your wife, you were also seen by him to stare *directly* at his window. In the middle of the night, across an alley that's at least twenty feet wide, one that doesn't have any lights, a dark alley. How did you know that there was a window there, Mr Sullivan? How did you know what to look at?'

There was no response from Robert Sullivan, but I saw Edith Sullivan keep her head high and place a firm hand on her husband's arm in support.

Maity laughed a little and looked at me. Then he said: 'The morning after Sayantan Kundu had come to see us, do you remember, Prakash, what I had told you about the photographs of Mr and Mrs Rajbanshi making love to each other? I had told you that they were very erotic! *That's* the one thing that was bothering me. *That* was my hunch. Real life is hardly that photogenic. In real life, when you see a murder happen, you don't see the victim swinging her arms frantically. You see her tear her assailant's face apart, or—in most cases—just lie there in shock! In real life, you see punctual and disciplined people. But you never see people who function like clockwork! In real life, an act of lovemaking will never, ever look so erotic, unless the focus is on *drawing your attention to it*.'

'What are you trying to imply, Maity?' I asked, my voice trembling at the prospect of the realization that he was trying to hint at. Could it be true? Could it? But . . . but . . . it was impossible!

'You know what I am trying to say, my friend,' Maity said. 'Because you felt it in your bones, too. It's just that you didn't think it was even possible. It was too daring, too fantastic, too outrageous an act to pull off!'

Impossible! Simply impossible!

'Dollhouse!' said Maity, in a whispering voice, 'Sayantan Kundu was watching a dollhouse through his camera! Six rooms, six frames! Everything he was seeing was being *fed* to him. Every single guest he was watching and photographing were nothing but puppets. Actors! Carefully placed in specific spots to serve one and only one purpose!'

No, no, no! This was impossible! What Maity was suggesting just couldn't be true!

'But why?' I almost cried out. 'To what purpose?'

Janardan Maity came and stood in the centre of the room. The words he then said seemed to echo through the room, making my head reel.

'The murder of Edith Sullivan by her husband was staged, Prakash! And every single person in this room who was staying at the Fairy Glen that night played an important, carefully thought-out, carefully written role in this unthinkable, unimaginable murder scene! A murder that was meant to be a distraction. A distraction for *another* murder. A murder of the one guest from the Fairy Glen who isn't here tonight. Yes! The murder of Harish Jhunjhunwala. Early this morning, the police found his corpse in an abandoned wasteland in the eastern fringes of the city, throat slit open. At the exact moment when Sayantan was watching the fake murder of Edith Sullivan, Harish Jhunjhunwala was being murdered in full view of Sayantan's camera in his room by none other than Mr T. Subramaniam! The police may have taken only a cursory glance at your work, Mr Subramaniam! But I, Janardan Maity, took care to read all of it. You were writing gibberish. Page after page of gibberish. It made no sense at all. You only wanted to *show* Sayantan Kundu that you sat at your desk all day and wrote your novel. Month after month after month. To such an extent that you became a boring subject for him. *That* was your alibi. You are the one who planned this entire thing. You are the puppet master in this devious, dangerous and heinous game. You pulled off the greatest magic trick that I have ever seen! And from one magician to another, I can tell you that you had successfully managed to make a fool out of everyone! But not me, Mr Subramaniam, not me! You cannot make a fool out of Janardan Maity!'

[18]

There was a stunned silence in the room. The guests looked at each other in a strange way. There was a mix of shock, apprehension, disbelief and confusion on everyone's faces. Only T. Subramaniam had a gentle smile of reverence playing on his face. I looked at Satish, his jaw had dropped too. It was he who broke the silence.

'I don't understand, Mr Maity,' he said. 'This does not make any sense at all!'

'It makes perfect sense, Satish,' said Maity. 'But only if you think about it from the perspective of the mind of a true genius! A master criminal!'

Maity now turned towards T. Subramaniam and said: 'He is *not* a writer at all. His claim to be a writer is part of his act. Think about it for a second, Prakash. I had told you there was something fishy about the entire thing, but you had credited it to the flow of thoughts and ideas of a writer. At that point of time, I could see that you were so convinced with that possibility that it would have been futile to argue with you. Moreover, your arguments were coming from a personal place, not from a logical one. It was coming from the fact that you yourself are a writer, and hence, by definition, knew better about the act of writing than I did. Which is true!'

I didn't know what to say. Maity had known all along! But he never once discussed it with me. And I now saw that it was all my doing. I was the one who had told him sternly that when it came to writing, I knew better than him.

'But what I was trying to tell you that day was about the *way* he was writing. You see like an act of lovemaking, like the habit of punctuality and discipline, and like a murder, the act of writing too is hardly that photogenic! Unless it is *staged*! Staged in a way that a writer simply sits at his or her desk and writes away! You, of all people, will vouch for the fact that writing involves long durations of thinking, editing, frustrations, distractions and several things *other* than writing. But I could see that day that you were not willing to believe that. Despite knowing it to be true, you didn't want to believe that, and do you know why? Because we all have an ideal *image* of writing in our heads. We all have an ideal *image* of lovemaking in our heads. An *image* of what a disciplined person would look like! Unknown to yourself, you have this image, this perception too. As did Sayantan. Subramaniam's genius was that he played on this perception, and staged the perfect image! A writer writing away. There's nothing interesting there. A man who functions like clockwork! After some time, he too will become boring. So then, what *is* interesting? The answer was always staring us in the face from inside the honeymoon suite! That's where Sayantan was *forced* to look. And then, while watching them, what does he see? He sees the couple have heard something. Something suspicious. He follows them. They can't see. *But he can!* The power a voyeur feels over the lives of others can be a dangerous, dangerous drug. Sayantan Kundu had fallen prey to this powerful narcotic. He sees a couple in the room downstairs quarrelling.

It comes to blows. The husband storms out. The wife cries herself to bed. The perfect image of a domestic quarrel! The couple upstairs have gone to sleep. That story is over. Their photographs have been taken. Where is the next story supposed to come from?'

We all looked at Maity as he spoke to us like a teacher speaking to a class full of enthralled students.

'Yes! From the Sullivans' room! Later that night, Robert returns, pretends to kill his wife, even puts up an act of taking his wife's corpse out of the room. But before he does that, before he leaves, he stares directly at Sayantan's camera. What is Sayantan's most natural reaction, under the circumstances? He hides. He takes his eyes off his camera. And at that precise moment, T. Subramaniam enters Harish Jhunjhunwala's room and slashes his throat.'

Everyone looked at Subramaniam, who did not react at all. Other than a calm smile on his face, there was no response from him to Maity's bizarre explanation.

'Wait a second,' I said. 'But why did he do all this? What is the motive here? And why would Jhunjhunwala open his door to Subramaniam? He was hiding, never opened his door to anyone.'

Maity smiled at me, 'You haven't got it yet, have you? Harish Jhunjhunwala too was one of Subramaniam's actors! He knew Subramaniam even before he had checked into the Fairy Glen. And it was only because Jhunjhunwala knew him that he opened the door to him. Little did he know what vicious plans Subramaniam had for him!'

'But . . . but why?' I almost cried out. 'Why did Subramaniam do all this? What is the motive here?'

Maity nodded and said: 'In order to truly understand why Subramaniam went to the lengths of planning this elaborate farce, we must first try and understand who he is. A simple back-of-the-envelope calculation will tell you that Subramaniam had spent lakhs of rupees on his stay at the Fairy Glen! Lakhs, not thousands! I was curious—where was he getting all this money from? Certainly not from his writing; he had told us he was unpublished. So I did a little bit of digging around. Thanks to my sources, I learnt that Subramaniam was the only son of a famous industrialist, one of the most affluent men in the country, based out of Chennai! And here he was—the sole heir to such a vast fortune—living in a dingy little dump like the Fairy Glen, in Kolkata. I asked myself—why?

'That's when I learnt that Subramaniam had absolutely no interest in his father's empire. And that he enjoyed living a Bohemian life—the life of an artist. He has lived in several cities in India. Tried to paint, sculpt, learn music. But he would soon get bored and move on. It is my belief that he was searching for something. Perhaps something incredible to do. My friends at the library told me he was a voracious reader, that he read on all subjects—including a subject that is quite close to my heart: *magic!* Perhaps his genius mind was craving to create something so remarkable, so unimaginably outrageous that his name would leave a mark in history. It is in this search, this journey, that a year or so ago, he arrived in Kolkata and put up at the Fairy Glen. And that is when he made a remarkable discovery! After a stormy night, he saw a man shooting photographs of the rooms of the Fairy Glen!

'Subramaniam realized that along with other guests of the hotel, he was being watched too. He found the entire phenomenon quite interesting, even appealing. Sayantan Kundu was watching T. Subramaniam in his room at the Fairy Glen. But outside the hotel, it was Subramaniam who began watching Sayantan Kundu. On the sidewalk, in the café, out on the street, in the market. They were taking turns to be the voyeur and the victim, with only *one* of them knowing what was going on! It was a strange, twisted game of cat and mouse. But only one of them was playing the other, taking him for a ride, so to speak. Knowing fully well that he was being watched by Sayantan, T. Subramaniam would put up an act of writing!

'But soon, he started to get bored of this game too. He had mastered this so well, that he wanted to move on and do something different, something even more outrageous. That's when a bizarre idea cropped up in Subramaniam's mind. If he had been able to successfully convince Sayantan that he—T. Subramaniam—was the victim of Sayantan's voyeurism, then why not extend the game? Take it to the next level? Get other people involved? What if the voyeur is made to believe that he saw something, when, in fact, he was seeing something entirely different? In other words, what if the voyeur is shown *an illusion*? And how far could this illusion go?

'Do you remember, Prakash? The night that Sayantan had come to see us, I had told you that magic was dying? Not in Subramaniam's mind, it wasn't. He decided to create the perfect magic trick and the perfect murder—both rolled into one! In many ways, a murder is like a magic trick, if you think

about it. There's the magician—the murderer. The pigeon—
the victim. And of course, the spectator—the detective! The
magician makes the pigeon vanish, and the detective must
work out how! And just as with a good magic trick, the
perfect crime is one that is simple. One that happens right
in front of your eyes—and *yet*, you don't see it. Because you
are looking elsewhere! When the magician is waving his wand
at the hat where you *thought* he put the pigeon, the bird is
in reality hidden up his sleeve! Robert and Edith Sullivan's
room was the hat! Harish Jhunjhunwala's room was the
magician's sleeve!'

'Mr Maity!' said Satish with a bit of impatience in his
voice. 'All this is quite theoretical, if you don't mind my saying
so. Can you tell us how he actually did it?'

'Sure,' said Maity, 'I believe the first thing Subramaniam
would have done was the first thing that I did—draw up a
diagram! Am I correct, Mr Subramaniam?'

All eyes turned towards T. Subramaniam who didn't say
a word, merely smiled.

'I'll take that as a yes,' said Maity. 'He then laid his plans
carefully. You see, our eyes, which can be compared to a ball,
move in two principal directions. Up–down. And left–right.
The average human being rarely rolls his eyes, and when he
does so, it is in fact a combination of movement along these
two axes. Up–down. Left–right. But never diagonally across.
Now look at this diagram. Subramaniam puts his victim in the
top left of the six rooms. That's his sleeve! And he puts the
distraction in the bottom right. That's his hat! The maximum
possible distance in a rectangular frame. A diagonal! And
what is the distraction? A fake murder!'

'But what was the guarantee that Sayantan Kundu would look at the Sullivans' room?' I asked. 'What was the guarantee that he would be distracted?'

'Aha!' said Maity, 'That's where the wand comes in! The wand that lures the audience's eye and tells them to look at the hat! The oldest, the most primeval, of all lures—sex!'

Maity now turned towards Kishore and Riya Rajbanshi.

'I believe your mother told my friend Prakash about a portfolio, Mrs Rajbanshi?' said Maity. 'This is the portfolio she was referring to, wasn't she? It has your photographs, your agent's contact details, everything. And it's all available on the Internet.'

Maity held up a few photographs in his hand and it was quite evident that both Kishore and Riya had recognized them.

'Subramaniam's biggest problem was: Who would he put in the honeymoon suite? Who would agree to play a sex scene on camera? The answer was simple. A porn star! When he came across the films that Mrs Rajbanshi had acted in, it was not very difficult for him to trace her down. But here's something that perhaps even he hadn't expected—he didn't even have to look for two actors! Imagine his delight when he came to know that you only work with each other! And money? Oh, that he didn't lack. He could pay you obscene amounts of money. All that you had to do was to follow a carefully written script.

'Oh yes! That bit of acting that you put on, of bringing the glass from the bathroom and trying to listen to what was going on in the room downstairs. *That* was the wand in Subramaniam's magic trick! That was when he was saying to his audience—look here! *This* is where the magic is happening.

And indeed, it worked! Sayantan saw the Sullivans quarrelling. He even saw Bob Sullivan punch his wife. That was a real punch by the way! The Sullivans are a financially needy couple. Robert, by his own admission, can't keep a job. Edith tries her best to keep the household together. Those words of Robert still ring in my ears: "Edith—she's the clever one"!'

I looked at Edith Sullivan and saw tears roll down her cheeks. Robert Sullivan was staring blankly at the floor. I somehow felt bad for them.

'I must admit one failure of mine though,' Maity said. 'One explanation that I cannot give you in this room today. And that is *how* Subramaniam met his actors. That is something that I don't know, nor will I ever know. He had time. He had one whole year to prepare, to write his script, to recruit his actors. What would a man in his position and with that vile objective do, I wonder? Roam around the city, walk its streets, sit in seedy cafés and tea stalls, observing, watching, listening to people? He handpicked his puppets— one by one! He must have thrown an obscene amount of money at each of them. The Sullivans too. A sum that Edith couldn't even think of in her wildest dreams. That's when she must have said yes and convinced Bob to play the role of the fake killer.'

'But wasn't there any risk involved for them?' I asked. 'Why would they agree to do this?'

'It is here that I have another wild, wild hypothesis,' said Maity. 'It is as wild as it is scary. It gives me the chills just to think about it. But I am willing to bet my last penny on the fact that it is true. It is my belief that Subramaniam never actually told any of his actors what his real intentions were.'

'He did *not*!' cried out Riya Rajbanshi, even as her husband tried to stop her. 'Otherwise I would have never, ever agreed to do this. This . . . this is *wrong*!'

Jayant Sinha too grunted and cussed under his breath, shaking his head, casting a furious glance at Subramaniam.

Maity said: 'Nor did he ever introduce any of his actors to each other, never told any of them what the other was doing, what role he or she was playing in this twisted game. For Sinha and Jhunjhunwala, the ask was simple enough. One had to stick to the clock, the other had to simply sit in his room and watch TV all day! A massive sum of money, for a seemingly simple task. Neither of them could say no to that! For Edith and Robert Sullivan, there was indeed a bit of a risk. But Subramaniam must have told them a simple solution. That if anything went wrong, if the police suspected Robert of having committed an actual murder, all that Edith had to do was to appear before them! The law, as I had said once to you, Satish, is a strange thing! It looks at evidence and *only* evidence! Now do you see why I had insisted that you let Robert Sullivan go? I knew Edith would come. *She* was the final piece of my puzzle!'

Satish nodded, and from the soft and almost invisible smile at the corner of his lips, I could tell that his respect for Maity had increased at least a thousandfold.

Maity was still speaking, 'Subramaniam thought that if something went wrong with the Rajbanshis, if Kishore or Riya tried to back out of his plan, he would be able to threaten them with the fact that they acted in pornographic films. And that's what Kishore Rajbanshi is so afraid of.'

I looked at the young man—he had buried his head in his hands.

'Kishore has seen poverty,' Maity went on. 'He was the one who was more afraid. He didn't want to go back to that life! And Subramaniam knew this. No wonder he was Subramaniam's trump card. Riya is the fiery one, also the more intelligent among the two, if I may say so. That brilliant act that you put up when Prakash was questioning you at your home—yes, I heard all about it. It was all improvised, on the spot! Extempore! Because neither you nor the man who hired you knew that Prakash would come looking for you. And from the way Prakash described the conversation he had with you, I could only doff my hat to you. May I say something to you, Mrs Rajbanshi?'

Riya Rajbanshi looked at Maity with teary eyes. Maity's voice was soft and gentle, 'You are an excellent actress, madam!'

Riya Rajbanshi broke down and collapsed on her chair. Kishore immediately hugged her and tried to console her.

'As are you, Mrs Sullivan!' said Maity. 'You wanted to be somebody! A model, a singer, an actress! You had fine taste, you had dreams, as your loving husband so beautifully put it. It was that aspiration, that unfulfilled aspiration of putting up an act in front of a camera and getting paid a handsome amount for it too that made you accept Subramaniam's offer. This man used you! All of you! He manipulated you, lured you with money. And why? Just to satisfy a twisted whim of his.'

Malcolm Brennan now spoke up, 'Mr Maity, I knew nothing of all this.'

'No, you didn't,' said Maity. 'But there was something you said when I was talking to you the other day that caught my attention. Do you remember that when we were talking about drunken brawls at the Fairy Glen, you had said that guests often carried their intoxicated friends and partners out

on their shoulders? Who better to have observed that than
the one man who has been staying in your hotel for the last
several months? Who better to know your precise schedule—
when you are at the counter, when you are away—who better
to have knowledge of that than Subramaniam?'

Malcolm Brennan gritted his teeth and looked at
Subramaniam whose eyes were still fixed on Maity.

'Poverty!' Maity went on, 'Taboo! Fear! Weariness! These
are only some of the weaknesses that Subramaniam played
upon to pull the strings of his puppets. Those, and one more.'

Maity's eyes swept across the room and came and stopped
at Jayant Sinha. 'Sheer stupidity!'

For the first time since Maity had exposed him, I saw
Subramaniam react. He laughed at what Maity had just said
about Jayant Sinha.

'You, Mr Sinha, were the clown of the act. Unknown
to yourself, you were. Someone whose presence is taken for
granted. Someone who is so predictable, that he is boring.
Someone who is *not* to be paid attention to. Someone who
Sayantan wouldn't even bother looking at. And finally,
someone who—if things went wrong—can be blamed for
the entire thing!'

'What do you mean, Maity?' I asked.

'Well, firstly,' said Maity, 'Sinha was the man who
Subramaniam had set up as someone who arrived at the hotel
and left on specific dates every month. So how do you create
suspicion? By making him *break* his routine. By making him
overstay. If, by chance, the police were to get involved, if
they started investigating, Sinha's departure from his regular
schedule would seem suspicious to them!'

Jayant Sinha was fuming; he now gave Subramaniam a death stare.

'And secondly?' I asked.

'Secondly,' Maity went on, 'these binoculars were Subramaniam's. High on magnification, narrow field of view. The first more important for Subramaniam than the second, as he watched Sayantan. But this was also the only thing connecting him to Sayantan's murder, and hence to this elaborate game that he was playing. So, when he finds out that I am investigating, what does he do? He gifts these binoculars to his clown! Who happily accepts them! Not knowing what the big picture is! Not knowing that he was getting involved in something as serious as murder!'

'But why Harish Jhunjhunwala?' asked Satish. 'Why him, specifically?'

'Two reasons,' Maity raised two fingers. 'First. He doesn't step out, doesn't let anyone into his room, doesn't answer his door. There had to be a perfectly reasonable explanation for that sort of behaviour, just in case the police started investigating. And who better than a man running from the law to fit that profile?'

My head was still reeling, thinking about the deviousness of the man's perverted mind. Even the way he was now looking at Maity gave me the creeps.

'Second,' continued Maity, 'I believe that during his search for the most ideal victim of his murder, Subramaniam must have spent some time with Harish. He knew he was a couch potato, a slacker. Sat in his couch and watched TV all day! In other words, someone who wouldn't be moving around in the room too much. Or, in other words, someone—and

I shudder to even think of this—whose *absence* of movement around the room wouldn't be noticed as something abnormal!'

'What are you saying, Maity?' my voice trembled.

Maity let out a deep sigh and said, 'I am saying, my friend, that for two days after his throat was slit, Harish Jhunjhunwala's corpse sat in his couch, facing a running television, in full view of Sayantan!'

'And Sayantan never noticed?' I gasped.

'And Sayantan never noticed!' said Maity. 'He didn't have any reason to. It was perfectly natural of Harish to spend hours on his couch. Subramaniam had successfully made Sayantan Kundu his most macabre victim of voyeurism!'

Even a seasoned man like Satish Mukherjee now rubbed his face with his palms. Everyone else in the room were breathing heavily. Subramaniam's sinister eyes—still smiling—were fixed on Maity.

'Two nights after the murder,' said Maity.

'Subramaniam simply walked out of the hotel with Harish Jhunjhunwala's corpse. And Malcolm Brennan didn't stop him. Why? Because he was taking a nap in the room behind the reception. Nor did he have any concern or alarm about the fact that Jhunjhunwala had disappeared. Why would he? Jhunjhunwala's room had been paid for much longer than he stayed! Subramaniam's plan was foolproof. He had thought of everything.'

'Dirty swine!' Malcolm Brennan cussed Subramaniam, who didn't pay any attention to him.

'Mr Maity,' Satish now said, 'does it not seem strange to you that a man—no matter how demented—would go to such great lengths to commit such a dangerous crime? One in which he ran the serious risk of being seen, and even photographed, *while* he was committing a murder?'

'Don't forget the macabre display of his trophy corpse, Satish!' said Maity. 'In full view! It's all there. Right in front of you. And *yet*, you cannot see it. You seem surprised by it, in fact you all do. But I am of the opinion that T. Subramaniam is the perfect example of a classic exhibitionist, an illusionist and a murderer—all rolled into one. I am also of the opinion that ordinary people such as you and I will not be able to truly comprehend the nature of his crimes. Not one, mind you, but *two* murders. Don't forget the murder of Sayantan Kundu! When he found out that I was investigating—something that he had just not expected to happen—he panicked. He realized that my character was not written in his script, although the police may well have been. He wondered if I would see what others had failed to see in Sayantan's photographs. That's when he murdered Sayantan, just to scare me away, or even divert my attention. Didn't you, Mr Subramaniam? But you see, I don't scare so easily! Nor can my attention be diverted, or my eyes fooled. Because like I said, I used to be a magician myself. I can see through your tricks. You won't be able to take me for a ride so easily, even if you tried to.'

'On the contrary, Mr Maity,' said T. Subramaniam in a gentle, respectful voice, 'from one magician to another, I have only the highest amount of respect for you. For everything that you just said. It . . .'

Subramaniam struggled to catch his breath and control his emotions, even as his eyes teared up.

'It takes an unthinkable, unimaginable amount of intelligence to do what you have done here today, Mr Maity. My respects, sir!'

Subramaniam rose from his chair and bowed to Maity. All of us in the room watched this strange spectacle. Maity simply watched the man. Calmly.

'Well,' said Subramaniam, 'that's about it, then! It was an enriching experience. Truly enlightening! Thank you, sir, for the evening. It's sad that it has to come to an end. But that's something that we can't avoid now, can we? Life goes on!'

Subramaniam picked up his book and his bag and prepared to leave. I looked at Maity and Satish in turns.

'Do something, Maity?' I said, exasperated. 'Satish?'

Both Maity and Satish's faces looked serious and grave. They didn't say anything by way of a response.

'We aren't going to let him walk away like this, are we?' I couldn't believe my eyes.

'You aren't such a great writer after all, Mr Ray,' said Subramaniam, calmly. 'This is not one of your detective novels, where the sleuth gives a rambling explanation to a room full of people at the end, describing how the crime was committed, and then the murderer goes and jumps at the detective's throat, thereby proving that all the hypotheses against him—mere conjectures thus far, and therefore not acceptable in a court of law—were indeed true! No, sir! Nothing of that sort is going to happen in this room tonight. You say that I recruited these people, Mr Maity? Asked them to play some kind of role in this illusion—as you describe it? Well, I am going to have to contest that. I have never met any of them before, let alone having any conversation with them.'

'You and I both know that's not true,' said Maity.

'Sir, sir, sir!' Subramaniam shook his head. 'Please don't speak like the rest of these people, sir! You're not one of them! You and I—we have a gift! Let's not trivialize that, instead, let's celebrate it! Why, for instance, will this, what's his name, Jhunjhunwala fellow listen to me and check into the Fairy Glen?'

'For money, Mr Subramaniam!' said Maity. 'It was easy money for him!'

'Oh, your claims are preposterous!' said Subramaniam. 'But you don't have any proof that he knew me, do you?'

Everyone looked at Maity, who hesitated for a few seconds. Then he said, 'Not exactly proof, but once again, a hunch!'

'Indeed?' Subramaniam smiled. 'A hunch? And what exactly is this hunch of yours?'

Maity said: 'Mrs Daisy Zorabian complained of disturbances from the room next door. And we all assumed that it was the honeymoon suite she was talking about. But how can that be? Because Kishore and Riya Rajbanshi checked into their suite *after* Mrs Zorabian had checked out. When she heard the noises, the honeymoon suite was vacant!'

The smile on T. Subramaniam's face wavered. His face looked pale for a few seconds.

'I'll tell you what must have happened,' continued Maity. 'Room 302 is an interesting room. Despite being vacant, I have always found it drawing my attention. And I wondered why! Until I realized its true purpose. To offer a screen between the room where all the action was happening—namely the honeymoon suite—and the room where the real murder was to take place. Therefore, according to Subramaniam's plan, that room should have been vacant and dark. That's what he had expected, because he knew exactly when the previous guest staying in that room would check out, that's how he had hatched his plan—around that bit of information. But, that was not to be. On nineteenth June, Malcolm Brennan gave the room to Mrs Zorabian. This upset Subramaniam's plan. The murder was supposed to take place that very night. Everyone had been given their roles, things had been set in motion, the wheels were turning and time was ticking away. What could Subramaniam do?

'That's when he realized that he would have to get Mrs Zorabian out of Room 302. By hook or by crook. He decided to create some sort of a disturbance by asking one of his actors to make some noise in their room. But think about it for a second! None of his actors were in their room at that time! The honeymoon couple hadn't checked in yet. The Sullivans didn't share a wall with Room 302—nor did Subramaniam himself. Jayant Sinha was out selling encyclopaedias, as per his routine, he would come back only later that evening. Who was the only actor available? Harish Jhunjhunwala! Subramaniam calls him—on his cell phone. Asks him to increase the volume of his television set! Jhunjhunwala does! The job is done!'

Satish and I exchanged glances. Subramaniam smiled lightly and said, 'Brilliant! As expected, brilliantly worked out! But not enough, Mr Maity! Not enough for the courts. That is also something that we have to think of, don't we? The court needs hard evidence. Proof! Where do you think you are going to get that from? You want to take the statements of these people? Very well! Go right ahead! I'll wait.'

I looked at the guests, as they hung their heads one by one. Jayant Sinha, Kishore Rajbanshi, Priya Rajbanshi, Robert and Edith Sullivan—none of them spoke up.

'I'll wait,' said Subramaniam. 'For a pornographic actress to testify against me. Knowing fully well that she and her husband and her mother will all go to jail if she does that. I'll wait for the Sullivans to speak up. Knowing that they won't get a penny if they do, and will have to continue with their wretched, barren, miserable lives till they are forced to pray for death to come and take them. I'll wait for this oaf of a man to testify against me so he can be dragged into jail for a crime that he could never muster the courage to commit—the crime of taking your life, Mr Ray! These people . . . people like these . . . they don't speak up, sir! They don't have a voice! You, of all people, ought to know that. They walk through their lives without having made a single remarkable achievement. They don't have any contribution to the world! They merely survive . . . from one day to another.'

T. Subramaniam started walking towards the door, 'So unless you have something concrete against me, Mr Maity, I bid you farewell and humbly ask that I be allowed to leave. Like I said, I have only the highest amount of respect for you. It's been an absolute pleasure meeting you. You truly are a worthy challenger! A superlative opponent! You . . . you *see* everything! Like I do! And in that sense, we are very much alike, don't you think?'

'No!'

Maity's voice startled everyone in the room and made Subramaniam halt in his tracks. Very slowly, he turned around to face Maity.

'No?' Subramaniam looked amused and slightly taken aback.

'For three reasons, Mr Subramaniam!' said Maity. 'You and I are not alike for three reasons!'

'Really?' smiled Subramaniam. 'Three? And what are they?'

'First,' Maity's voice boomed and reverberated through the room as he slapped a photograph down on the table. 'I do not take human lives!'

All of us rose to our feet and looked down at the photograph on the table to find T. Subramaniam talking to Edith Sullivan. It was quite apparent from the photograph that the conversation was a heated one. I looked up at Subramaniam to find that the smile had vanished from his face.

'Second,' Maity's voice echoed through the room again, as he slapped another photograph on the table. 'I do not use simple, poor, innocent people to commit heinous crimes!'

The second photograph showed T. Subramaniam shaking Kishore Rajbanshi's hand. I looked at both Kishore and Subramaniam. The blood seemed to have drained from their faces.

'And finally,' Maity's roar was so potent that it shook the room, even as he slapped yet another photograph on the table. 'I do not take credit for things I have not done!'

The third and final photograph showed Subramaniam giving the binoculars Maity had shown us to Jayant Sinha, and Sinha smiling at him.

'These . . . these . . . photographs . . .' Subramaniam stammered.

'From one magician to another, Mr Subramaniam,' roared Maity. 'Allow me to show you one last magic trick before you leave! A trick that you will never forget your *entire* life!'

As Maity pointed towards the door of the interrogation room, the constable opened the heavy door with a thunderous clang, and in walked a man with a familiar face and a familiar smile.

Impossible! This was impossible!

Sayantan Kundu!

Before he collapsed on the floor in a faint, Subramaniam must have heard one final word in Maity's voice thundering through the interrogation room that evening. The rest of us sure did.

'Abracadabra!'

[19]

Trinca's on Park Street always had a fond, soothing effect on me. The restaurant had a calm and tranquil ambience with its soft lighting and muted décor, not to mention the delicious food. So, after walking out of Park Street Police Station, when Maity asked me where I wanted to go for dinner, I said: Trinca's. Maity agreed on one condition—that it would be his treat. The three of us—and by three I mean Maity, Sayantan Kundu and I—walked the short distance to Trinca's. One good thing about Kolkata is that no matter how hot and humid the city gets during the summer day, there is always the cool evening breeze blowing from over the river to calm everything down. Even now, as we walked on the wide sidewalks of Park Street, Maity and Sayantan a little ahead, I a little behind, a river of traffic flowing past me on what was arguably the busiest street in the city, I felt the evening breeze cooling me down. An inexplicable sense of melancholy had descended on me. I knew this feeling very well. It often came after Janardan Maity had successfully solved an intricate mystery. And I found it strange because every time he did, I only expected a sense of euphoria, a sense of victory to prevail upon me. But no! It was always a sense of sadness, as if there was a vacuum, an emptiness left behind. As if a part of me had vanished from my life forever.

We didn't have a reservation but were lucky to find a table for three—that too by the side of the street, along the glass façade of the iconic restaurant. We ordered a few appetizers; Sayantan asked for a beer, and we settled down in our seats.

'Too bad Satish couldn't come,' said Maity. 'I'd asked him, but he said he would be too busy now. "You've done your job," he said, "now my work begins."'

Sayantan smiled and looked at me. I stared back at him, with a vague, blank expression.

'I'm assuming you have questions, my friend,' said Maity.

'Maity . . .' I began, but was promptly stopped by my dear friend.

'I am sorry, Prakash,' he said. 'As I said to you once before, I hope you will forgive me. The less people knew the better it was. This entire thing would have been for nothing if I hadn't introduced a little chaos into Subramaniam's plan. His well-oiled puppets, his carefully written script, his setting, his financial power—everything was perfect! Just perfect! But there was one thing that he did not have, in fact, could not possibly have had. And that was trust. He did not trust his puppets. And that is why, when I put up the entire drama of Sayantan's murder with the help of Satish, and the news reached his ears, he was rattled. Shaken, to the core. Because it was not part of his script. He must have wondered: Who murdered Sayantan? Who among his well-oiled, well-strung, carefully handpicked and cautiously-taught puppets could have done that? And panic was his biggest mistake. He tried to get in touch with all the key players of his game, to confirm if they had had any hand in Sayantan's murder. Because he knew, that *he* hadn't. And that is when he was followed and photographed. And who better to do that than a voyeur?'

'It was you, wasn't it?' I asked Sayantan. 'I recognized those photographs the moment I saw them.'

Sayantan nodded, 'Mr Maity warned me that what I was getting into would be dangerous. But he also said that he trusted me. I, in turn, trusted him. It all worked out in the end.'

I shook my head in disbelief, 'You used me as bait! Again!'

'Yes, I did,' said Maity in a gentle, apologetic voice. 'And I am sorry. But there was no other way. I wanted someone to rouse the arrogance in the man. And I myself couldn't do that. Nor could Satish. It was his arrogance that spelt his doom. Everything he said in that room, about never meeting or knowing anything about any of his players—that was in itself not enough to convict him. But along with these photographs, those words of his would be enough to put charges against him. I had control over the latter. But I had no control over his arrogance—he could have just kept his mouth shut. That was where *you* came in. I wanted you to *believe* that Sayantan had been murdered. And there was no better plan to make you believe that than to *stage* his murder! I played Subramaniam at his own game. His arrogance did the rest.'

I thought for a few seconds and said: 'Whatever we have against him, will it be enough?'

'You mean to put him in prison?' Maity asked. 'Men like Subramaniam do not rot in prisons, Prakash. His father will hire the best of lawyers, use all his powers, connections, wealth and muscle to save his only child. Not a single word of what happened in the Fairy Glen will ever be published or broadcast in the media. No one will ever know.'

'Except the few of us?' I asked.

Maity nodded, 'Except the few of us. I also have a strong feeling about something else. A hunch!'

Maity's voice had changed. I asked, 'And what is that?'

Maity stared in the void and remained silent for a while. Then he said, 'I have a feeling that we will meet again! Subramaniam and I. That man—Satish and his entire police force would never be able to truly comprehend what a devilish genius that man is! How his mind works. What excellent knowledge of human psychology he has! What exceptional intelligence his brain possesses! That little trick he pulled, when he made Robert Sullivan stare directly at Sayantan's window—what a masterstroke that was!'

We sat in silence for a long time. I felt that sense of melancholy overpowering me yet again. I looked around the restaurant to find people chatting and conversing between their meals—people from all walks of life. I suddenly remembered Riya and Kishore Rajbanshi had planned to meet her father at Trinca's. Then I looked out of the glass wall and saw pedestrians on the sidewalk and vehicles on the road—hundreds and thousands of them, just passing by. Once again, I wondered what a strange tapestry life had woven—one in which the fortunes and miseries of people were intertwined. And at that moment I had the realization that the ordinary man on the street, the faces in the crowd—the millions and billions of people who walked through life merely in order to survive from one day to another—their contribution to the world was perhaps the most beautiful one. Their contribution was in their existence itself! In the fact that they had the courage to survive! That was no mean feat! It required guts to go out there every day and fight the battle of survival. The bloody, agonizingly painful battle to be able to see another sunrise. Subramaniam was wrong! Those men and women deserved applause—just for putting up that fight!

Maity slapped the table and said, 'Well, let's forget about all that and enjoy ourselves. I think it would be fair to say we earned it. And as if on cue, here comes the food!'

After our food and drinks had been served and we had dug in, Sayantan asked, 'What will happen to the other guests now? The puppets—as you call them?'

Maity said, 'I'm not quite sure. The law will take its course. Satish is looking into all that, it's his department. But I must admit I feel bad for them. None of them knew what they were getting into.'

'But I did!'

Maity and I stopped eating and looked up. Sayantan had said those words. And the way he said them made us look at him.

'A year ago, when that window pane shattered and I picked up my camera to look out of it, I knew what I was getting into,' continued Sayantan, hanging his head and smiling a little. 'Every single click of my shutter button—I knew. Without exception. I knew I was changing lives—forever. Causing irreparable harm to people. Committing a crime. If the Sullivans, the Rajbanshis and Jayant Sinha deserve their punishment, then so do I.'

I looked at Maity, he was staring at Sayantan Kundu's face.

'I have arranged for that too,' said Maity.

Sayantan Kundu looked up slowly.

'I have spoken to Satish Mukherjee and tomorrow morning, you will go and meet him in his office,' said Maity.

'There, you will give him the names, addresses and other details of all the people you have blackmailed and extorted money from over the last one year. And then, with his help, you will contact each of them, anonymously of course, and give them their negatives back, not to forget their money too.'

Sayantan was dumbstruck for a few seconds. Then he said, 'I . . . I'm absolutely willing to do that, Mr Maity. But there's only one problem . . . I . . . I don't . . .'

'Money?' Maity had picked up his fork and knife and dug into his chicken cutlet again. 'That won't be a problem. Consider it a loan from a friend. But I will insist that you pay me back. Live an honest life, earn it and pay me back.'

Sayantan Kundu looked at me in disbelief and I smiled at him. He didn't know my friend Janardan Maity well enough. I did!

'I can't thank you enough, Mr Maity,' he grabbed Maity's hand with a deep sense of gratitude. 'I'll repay every penny to you. But I don't think I can ever repay the debt of your forgiveness.'

'You are committing a worse crime than blackmailing innocent people right now,' Maity said. 'By stopping a hungry man from having Trinca's famous chicken cutlet in peace.'

Sayantan Kundu apologized and let go of Maity's arm. I laughed and was immediately startled by something I had seen outside the window on the footpath of the busy Park Street. A young boy was standing on the road by the window, his eyes focused on his palm, on which there were a few coins and currency notes, which he was busy counting. It was the young bellboy from the Fairy Glen. I realized someone must have given him a tip.

I drew Maity's attention to the boy. Maity's eyes shone and a smile appeared on his lips. He dropped his fork and knocked on the glass. The boy looked up and waved at us, flashing that beautiful smile of his. I recalled Malcolm Brennan had said all the guests loved him and that when he smiled, his eyes smiled too!

Maity waved at him and gestured at him to wait. The boy nodded.

'Sayantan,' said Maity, 'go bring him inside!'

Sayantan immediately walked towards the main door and Maity turned his attention back to his food.

'That was a good thing you did there,' I told him. 'With Sayantan.'

Between chewing his food, Maity said, 'Remember what I had told you? A little bit of luck, and just a little push. His luck is not in my hands. That was the push!'

I looked at Janardan Maity, busy eating. And once again, my respect for the man grew. I could not think of a single time in the past when he had had to solve so complex a mystery, so baffling a puzzle. And here he was, sitting at Trinca's, enjoying a simple meal. There was no arrogance in him, no bragging. Just sheer benevolence.

'Hello!'

The young boy had reached the table and greeted us.

'Hey, Chief!' said Maity. 'It's nice to see you again!'

'You didn't have to come get me,' said Chief. 'Everyone knows me around here!'

Maity smiled. Chief now turned towards Sayantan and said, 'I have seen you around. But hey, I heard you were dead!'

'In a way he was!' said Maity. 'Now he's back!'

Sayantan smiled. Chief didn't pay much attention to Maity's words. He was now looking at the table, where Sayantan had kept his camera.

'What kind of camera is this?' he asked, pointing at it.

'It's a Canon,' said Sayantan.

'What's this?'

'That's the shutter button. You press it when you want to shoot the photograph.'

'And this?'

'That's the viewfinder. You look through it to see what you are shooting, how your photograph will look.'

'Can I have a look?' Chief asked.

'Sure,' said Sayantan. 'Go ahead. Here, let me help you!'

Maity and I exchanged smiling glances as Sayantan picked up his camera, placed it in Chief's hands and put the strap around his neck. The young boy placed his eye on the viewfinder, pointed the camera at the small flower vase on the table and pressed the shutter.

'Wow!' he exclaimed.

'See?' said Sayantan, 'You're a natural at this!'

The boy turned the camera around a few times and then said, 'What's this?'

I looked at Maity, and so did Sayantan. Maity was smiling, patiently. He nodded ever so gently at Sayantan. Sayantan flashed a warm smile of gratitude at Maity and then turned towards the bright and inquisitive young boy.

'That's the aperture!' he said. 'That's from where the light comes in!'

Scan QR code to access the
Penguin Random House India website